Level Up

Kindle Alexander

ACKNOWLEDGMENTS

The author acknowledges the trademarked status and trademark owners of the trademarks mentioned in this work of fiction

Level Up has been fully edited by a team of trained editors but no manuscript is perfect. Please feel free to email me with any mistakes you find at kindle@kindlealexander.com

Creative license was taken with this story.
It is a work of fiction.

CONTENTS

DEDICATION

Kindle, I miss you.
Perry, we need you here.
Lee Rey, this one is on you.
Thank you for staying on us. Ducky deserves to be loved.

"Hesitation is defeat." ~ Shadows Die Twice

CHAPTER 1
THE BIG CHANGE

"I don't know. Are you sure?" Duncan Reigns, Ducky to his friends and family, asked. He glanced over his shoulder, eyeing his reflection in the full-length mirror sitting in the middle of the dressing room just off Greer Lockhart's large walk-in closet.

He turned a one-eighty, focusing on the style and cut of the suit he wore. When an answer didn't come, he lifted his gaze to find Greer studying the outfit as well. After a few tense moments, something close to satisfaction passed over Greer's stern face.

"Positive. But stop moving. You fidget constantly. Stop." Greer stepped toward Ducky, gripping his shoulders, pushing them back until they refused to go any further, forcing Ducky into the position he wanted. "You've got to stop slumping. Head up, shoulders back. Proper posture all the time. The reason you aren't satisfied with any of these clothes is because you're not owning them. They own you. It throws off the whole look. Whether or not you feel confident, you must present yourself as a man who not only owns nice clothing but also owns the space around him. Lift your chin, too. Stop looking down."

Ducky held the awkward pose, intentionally keeping his chest puffed out as he rotated around to look back into the mirror. The transformation in his appearance occurred instantly. His gaze drifted to Dallas, his brother, who leaned against the doorframe separating the dressing room from the main bedroom. Dallas's brawny biceps noticeably bulged with his arms crossed tightly over his chest.

Since Ducky had first mentioned the idea of Greer helping him with a total body makeover, Greer had taken the role as mentor and transformer to heart. He used strict guidance and a tight schedule with his tutelage and had zero qualms about correcting Ducky. He did it frequently.

After months of following Greer's drill sergeant approach to working out, Ducky's soft, almost nonexistent muscles had developed. The physical part hadn't come easy, but the rewards were worth it. Greer had finally moved this makeover in the direction Ducky had originally thought they'd start: his clothing. He'd always been impressed by the way Greer dressed. But now he understood it was more than just the clothes that made Greer, Greer.

Since they'd started, Ducky had become accustomed to living in a constant state of sore, aching muscles. Greer had changed his eating habits too. No more fast food. Not to worry, he still snuck in a cheeseburger or two whenever he got the chance. No one knew that truth. Or…at least Greer hadn't called him out on it.

Ducky could see for himself that he looked like a completely different man today because of Greer's unwavering guidance. Those five in the morning wake-up calls, pushing him out of bed to work out, never failed to motivate. He learned the hard way that if he didn't answer, Greer would get in his car and drive over. The workouts with Greer beside him were a million times harder than the ones he did alone.

His head was taking a little more time to adjust to the change. His confidence levels weren't elevating as quickly as he hoped. He still fought that inner voice that kept insisting this outer appearance was a ridiculous impostor. Per Greer, those insecurities weren't hidden. They spoke volumes in his poor posture and constant crossed arms over his chest. Ducky only agreed with Greer's first observation, not the second. He crossed his arms to give him something to do with his hands when he was forced out into the world with real people. If he didn't tuck them away, he'd fidget nervously. If he couldn't find the right words to say, he'd try to speak with his hands. Which turned into a whole-arm movement that eventually included his entire upper body, as if he planned to take flight with all the flapping he did.

Even now, he had a hell of a time just standing still with his arms hanging casually at his sides. He'd watched both Dallas and Greer cross their arms while thinking through a situation… With his shoulders still held back and his chest expanded in the unnatural pose, he carefully crossed his arms over his chest like Dallas's to test the look.

His focus riveted on the mirror, insistently noting the difference between the two looks. As he studied his posture, he gnawed on his lip, memorizing this exact stance. Honestly, he was proud of what he saw. Other than the unruly mop of curls on his head that had to be continually tossed aside to be able to see, he didn't look half bad.

"Tuck your fist under your bicep," Dallas instructed, drawing Ducky's attention. Dallas lifted a fist and pushed it back underneath his crossed arm, enhancing the look of his bicep.

"So, that's how you do that?" Ducky asked, amazed at the difference.

"You have much to learn, little one," Greer teased, chuckling as he turned away. Between where Ducky and Dallas stood lay a massive pile of men's clothing. Dozens of boxes of shoes, socks, and belts. All in every style and color imaginable. They littered the available space from the floor to the countertops to the towel racks, spilling into the large closet.

The chaos represented hours of wardrobe changes. Greer had never tired, even when Ducky thought he'd found his style after the first fitting and was ready to call it done.

"Now that we know what looks the best, it'll be easier to dress you from this point forward. You'll stick with that cut then add seasonal trends to help keep you looking like you belong on the cover of GQ. It's how I was taught to dress and do it every day. I like my clothes fitted and have since I first started deciding my own style. The colors and accessories keep me looking on trend," Greer explained as he gathered various discarded wrappings. Greer didn't tend to care about things out of place, but Ducky's brother didn't like a mess. That very personality trait left Dallas with little option to do anything more than push off the wall to pitch in to clean the normally tidy space.

Luckily for Ducky, he didn't have those clean-freak sort of hang-ups. The more clutter the better to hide the mess underneath.

"You've done the hard part. It gets easier from here, I promise," Dallas added, bending to sort through the different shoes dropped haphazardly into the boxes.

Ducky wasn't entirely sure he believed either one of them as he turned back to stare at himself in the mirror. Everything he'd endured over the last few months, from working out twice a day on StreamTrainer, to hiring a health-food oriented chef to teach him how to eat better, none of it had become normal. What a ridiculous notion to have someone preparing his meals in his tiny apartment.

Maybe he was more like a voyeur, destined to look down at his life, never fully connecting. He'd been coasting, disjointed, since his and Dallas's business had hit the big time.

As much as his own reflection in the mirror confused him, so did the idea of owning StreamTrainer, the most popular home workout device on the market today. The company had grown so big, so fast that everything else had become a blur. He had more money than he knew what to do with. Thank goodness for Greer and his investment knowledge. Except now that his money was making money....

Ducky's armpits began to sweat, and he pushed all those anxiety-filled thoughts aside. Thinking about his finances made his stomach hurt. He had always railed against the man he'd now become...

"I think it's time I tackle my hair," Ducky said absentmindedly, unbuttoning his suit coat. As he shrugged it off, he stepped away from the mirror. Both Greer and Dallas stared at him. Ducky's fingers barely caught the coat as it slid down his back, into his palms.

The astonishment staring at him caused a chuckle under his breath, understanding exactly what they were thinking. He'd hid behind the curtain of curls for most of his life. Not having a real haircut since junior high school, maybe before then. His hair only grew so far with every curl springing out like a coil. "I like the shorter sides with the hair waving out the front like Nick Champa or Pierre Bouvier."

Greer nodded and said, "Cute couple. That style's perfect for you."

Ducky hung his suit coat on a nearby towel hook, grinning. For all these months, he'd held firm against cutting his hair. If this makeover hadn't worked, then he wanted to keep the security of his frizzy mop. Dallas's fist popped into Ducky's peripheral vision. His brother had always been on his side. Dallas had looked out for Ducky his entire life. Maybe the only person in the world that believed Ducky had value. He extended a fist, meeting his brother's knuckles.

"Thank you," he mumbled, a little above a whisper. Dallas's warm gaze met Ducky's.

"Not me, thank you. You did this. You've accomplished so much."

The weight of emotion had him ducking his head as he unbuttoned his dress shirt and turned toward the closet, his changing room for the day. Dallas didn't let him get too far without gripping his shoulder and squeezing. He appreciated the encouragement as his phone's alarm reminded him of the time.

He had to go. He was in a *League of Legends* tournament that evening. The day should have been spent practicing for the game. He hoped he didn't fuck his team up.

The band of rebels he'd always played with insisted he'd given up his rebel card by giving into the establishment's view of normality. He couldn't help the grin as he shut himself in the walk-in-closet for privacy. His buddies weren't wrong, but they also didn't have a problem with all the sponsorships and free trips they got because of his deep pockets. Hell, most of them were employed by him these days. Capitalism couldn't be all bad.

"Yeah, I guess you're right, Dad." Defeat edged every syllable Chad Reeves muttered into the phone. The pause he'd given in packing his weekender resumed. Chad stuffed in the last few items for the quick, couple of day turnaround trip. He took a final glance around the room, searching for anything he may have forgotten. Tension tightened his neck and shoulders. His father never listened to him anymore.

All his childhood engrained manners of appreciation taught to him by his father and mother, Dylan and Teri Reeves, forced their way to the surface. He had to remember all the well-meaning gifts and gestures his father gave him. From this badass upper floor apartment in the middle of the Uptown area of Dallas, Texas, to the soft leather duffle bag he used to pack for this trip. All provided by his father and stepdad, Tristan Wilder, one of the richest men in the world, to ensure he had a comfortable life.

The guilt wrecked his mood even further. He was a selfish bastard for not eagerly accepting his father's help and moving on with his day. A heavy sigh slipped free as he plopped his ass down on the most expensive mattress on the market. It absorbed his body as if made just for him. Another nonnegotiable gift when he moved in.

"Tell me what's wrong?" Dylan asked. His tone indicated that he had finally tuned in, becoming present to the conversation, paying closer attention to Chad's mood.

What did he say that he hadn't said a hundred times over by now?

His inner truth didn't create a balance within him either. Wanting to be a self-made man, to have his own accomplishments, ones he earned himself, made him sound like an utter hypocrite. When he was younger, fresh out of high school and his dad had first come out, revealing his and Tristan's relationship, Chad had enjoyed riding on his stepfather's name and his own newfound local fame.

Seven years later, he couldn't escape the clamor of being a Wilder no matter how hard he tried. He recognized the visual cues a person gave once they realized who he was related to. Even finding real friends anymore had become near impossible. People always had some angle to try to get to Tristan.

"All right, I'm alone. I stepped outside. Now tell me what's wrong." Dylan tried again to get Chad to talk, this time lowering his voice as the sounds of the Southern California ocean filled the background.

"It's nothing, Dad. Forget it." That had to be a good enough answer for right now because the solutions to his problems wouldn't come easy.

Tristan had no biological children of his own and took to parenting like a kid in a candy store. He could easily be nominated the world's best stepfather. Nothing ever rattled the man. Tristan made it his life's goal to attend every one of Chad's golf tournaments. He traipsed after Chad, determined to show his support. In return, he created a frenzy for the paparazzi who followed the PGA tour wherever it went.

After so long, the newness of having a ready-made family should have worn off. Not for Tristan though. His limitless generosity and attention weren't going anywhere, making Chad's hard-earned personal achievements suspect to those competing against him. At least based on all the ribbing he took.

Honestly, it was messing with his head.

"Please…" his father's voice sounded concerned, even hurt. A lecture about the validity of feelings and Chad's truth being worthy was on its way if he didn't say something soon.

He anchored the phone between his ear and shoulder, getting to his feet. No one had time for all his self-pity. He zipped the bag closed as frustration hardened the already tightened muscles in his neck, shoulders, and back.

"Don't worry, Dad. I'm just being me. I feel like if Wilder Incorporated jumps in and sponsors me on the tour, then also sponsors the PGA, no one's gonna believe my skill earned my way there. I get that you're both proud I've made it this far. I appreciate your support, but I did this, Dad." Did he truly earn his successes or were they given to him because of Tristan's constant involvement?

There was no way to know for sure. Which sucked.

"We know you're a gifted athlete, son. Of course you did. Twenty-five years old and you've earned playing privileges. Tristan's happy for you. He wants to show his support. And it's not only about you. Wilder's expanding their physical fitness initiative. Something you started when you put StreamTrainer in front of us," Dylan reiterated, his voice lowering, putting all the weight back on Chad's shoulders. "I can tell him you'd rather not play under Wilder Sports."

Like always, Chad felt like a heel and his heart got in the

way. Tristan would pretend to understand but get his feelings bruised.

And the whole Wilder Sports concept was truly Chad's idea. He'd mentioned it over the holidays. A program to compete against Red Bull Sports. Tristan had fallen hook, line, and sinker.

Which reminded him of the exact reason for his upcoming trip in the first place. He had a plane to catch. Chad grabbed the bag strap and slung it over his shoulder as he pivoted toward his bedroom door. He grabbed his sunglasses, wallet, and passport. His flip-flops were kicked off right inside the entry. His packed surfboard waited by the shoes.

"Don't tell Tristan. I told you it's just me being me. I'll appreciate this at some point. Tell him I'm heading to Costa Rica to surf with Kai Maloney. I'll report back as soon as I know something."

His father's even breaths were the only thing breaking the silence on the other end of the phone, making him feel like a bigger jerk for being ungrateful.

"If you aren't interested in finding talent for WS, just tell Tristan. He only moved forward with the concept after you seemed on board with helping. You're a smart man. There's nothing he thinks you can't do. Tell him you don't want to be interim head of the project. Maybe one of the StreamTrainer brothers could take the lead in finding athletes until we hire someone. You don't have to be involved."

The mention of the StreamTrainer brothers caused Chad's heart to give a strange quiver. He'd known Ducky Reigns for years. Since they were boys playing *League of Legends* over Xbox together. He wasn't sure there were too many secrets Ducky didn't know about him. They were close in a way only gamers could understand. They had always been.

Moreover, Ducky was the only person who had never tried to use him for his family connection. Hell, Chad had even offered to put Ducky's new business in front of his dad. Chad had never done that for anyone else. He fought to ignore his body's sudden surge of desire at the mention of Ducky and switched his phone to his other hand to grab the surfboard.

The protective thing he did with Ducky was weird, but Chad had reconciled those feelings a long time ago. Talk about self-made, that was Ducky. Chad's bad mood took a deeper dive as he left his apartment, letting the door swing heavily shut behind him.

You're going down the Ducky rabbit hole right now. Focus.

"It's not that, Dad. I volunteered to go to Costa Rica. I think Kai's the kind of athlete to help start this up for us. Be our headliner."

"Tristan believes you're the first athlete to headline…" Dylan interrupted, taking the conversation full circle.

"I'm not ready to headline…" He might have made it into the PGA, but he hadn't done well there. His head wasn't in the game there either. His low scores and poor rankings were nowhere good enough to be the kind of talent Wilder needed to garner excitement for a professional sports program.

"What's going on?" Chad heard Tristan's deep tenor in the background on the other end of the phone. "Which child are you talking to?"

"Dad, I gotta go. I'm fine. Go on with your day. Tell Tristan thank you for the sponsorship, and I'll get back to him about my decision. I'll also send him the video of Kai as soon as I get out there with him. See ya." Chad took the opportunity to end the call before his father could say anything more. If he didn't, they'd go round and round until everyone was walking on eggshells around each other.

At the elevator bank, Chad pushed the call button with more force than necessary. The elevator door opened with the only other person in the car being his new neighbor on the twentieth floor. The one right above Chad's place. Everyone in the building was talking about her. He knew why. She was tall, blond, and had the kind of eyes that drew a person in. He stepped on with a smile tugging at the corners of his lips. His problems instantly forgotten.

CHAPTER 2
ON THE INSIDE

"Sir, can I help you?" Ella, the receptionist at the front desk of StreamTrainer, asked as Ducky walked through the crowded front foyer, heading to his office. Business had grown too fast to stay on top of appropriate office space for their employees. Desks with small partitions filled every available square inch of the corporate office, including the front lobby. Eight customer service representative workspaces surrounded the entry, circling Ella's large, modern reception desk.

Every employee's head turned in his direction. The constant low-level chatter of the reps fielding their calls became silent.

"I'm going to the office," Ducky muttered, pointing in that direction, never stopping his well-worn path to the administrative office he now shared with Skye and Dallas.

"Sir, you have to have an appointment," Ella called out, her chair squeaking as she got to her feet and circled around the desk to follow. Only when entering his office did he glance back over his shoulder, cocking a questioning brow.

"Can I help you?" Skye asked, snapping Ducky's attention to her as she rose from one of the three desks in the office. She looked confused, laying the landline phone in its cradle. Their gazes connected and held.

"I'm Ducky. Duncan Reeves. I work here," he said, tapping his chest as he stepped further inside the office to let the receptionist follow him in. Did Greer set this greeting up as some sort of prank? He looked down the length of his body. Today was the first day he chose to wear something new, a pair of fitted jeans and a tight vintage Slash T-shirt, the only purchase he'd been allowed to make when adding to his new wardrobe.

His gaze shifted from Skye to the receptionist then back to Skye. Neither looked as if they understood the basic English coming out of his mouth. If they teased him, they were damn good. Like award-winning actresses.

Then a moment of clarity happened.

Skye's eyes widened with recognition. "Omigod, Ducky. What did you do to your hair?" she asked, coming around her desk, her facial features going through a rapid transformation of astonished expressions.

"Laura called it an undercut with um…" Heat flooded his cheeks. Why did he feel like he'd been put on the spot? He hadn't been prepared to answer questions about his new look. Talking about himself didn't come naturally. He always preferred blending into the background. Skye's fascination caught him absolutely off guard.

Ducky also wished he'd paid better attention to Laura so he sounded a little more knowledgeable. "I can't remember what she called the blow dry part. It was some kind of tropical blow out." He lifted his hand to his hair but stopped just short of touching the styled strands. Maybe that wasn't actually Skye's question. He wasn't any good at picking up people's emotional cues—another area he was trying to work on.

The moment grew more awkward by the minute. He should probably explain. Silence made him nervous. He felt as weird as the look on both of their faces. He shifted his weight, trying to distract himself from the fact that, by cutting his hair, he'd lost the only barrier that hid him from the world.

Maybe he should've gone home, gotten a better grip on this new look before coming to work. Either way, he couldn't stop the over explanation tumbling from his lips. "I wanted that big poof in the front look, but my hair's too curly. It'd take too much time to fix. I'll need to do that in baby steps. I figured it'd be hard since I haven't had to do my hair before…"

"Ducky." Thank God Skye interrupted him as he took a step back, his ass hitting the edge of Dallas's desk. He would have kept talking forever if she hadn't stopped him.

"Look at me." Skye placed both her palms on his cheeks to turn his face in her direction. A move he'd normally shy away from. He didn't really like people touching him, but Skye was family, at least in this modern-day friends to family world. "You're so handsome. This is the perfect style for your face. I don't think I've ever truly seen you before. Your jaw's so strong. You look like Dallas."

Her fingers traced the length of his jaw as her grin grew wider.

Heat flooded his cheeks again as he moved his face out of her hands. The sound of footsteps heading in the direction of the office made him instantly step back to put space between him and their employees spilling into the small room.

"It's not that big a deal. Y'all know Greer doesn't do anything halfway." The way he responded to Skye's compliment sounded lame even to him.

"This is a huge deal," Sara, who handled their marketing and public relations, said, plowing her way through the gathering crowd of stunned employees.

Privacy was an issue inside the crowded office space, but he hadn't realized that literally everyone in these front offices could hear every word spoken.

"You look great." She moved to the side of his desk, her gaze scanning the length of his body. "The clothes, the hair. You lost the half-growing beard. You're our next promotion. I can see the ads now. You go present at the game award show. Show yourself off, then we'll immediately follow with a nationwide ad campaign with your transformation. People have got to see what StreamTrainer can do for them. You're the company's owner. This is brilliant. How does your body really look? I can see the muscle definition through the T-shirt, but is it as defined as Dallas's? Can you teach some classes?"

Oh, dear God, no. Sara needed to stop talking that nonsense. She boldly leaned forward to lift the hem of his T-shirt. He pushed back to move away from the touch. How had they completely forgotten how he didn't like interacting with people? Nothing had changed.

He would never do an advertising campaign for any reason. He shook his head *no* as Skye both figuratively and literally jumped into the mix, bouncing up and down, adding her two cents to the idea. "I'm one hundred percent certain there's a hard body underneath those clothes. I haven't said anything because he's so private, but Dallas talks about how hard he's working out." Skye caught him off guard when she came around his desk and shoved the tee's sleeve up to reveal his entire bicep. Heat rushed over every part of his body as he flushed with embarrassment.

"This is why I don't tell y'all anything." Ducky swatted Skye's hand away. Laughter from the crowd that had gathered in the doorway made him add, "We have work to do. I hear the phones ringing. Go back to your jobs. This is ridiculous. Leave me alone." He reached for the edge of his office chair and sat. He Flintstoned his feet to drive his chair forward. He turned on his CPU, attempting to ignore them all. His system rivaled that of something inside an air traffic control tower. The comforting hum of the machines and multiple screens coming to life comforted him in its own way.

"We embarrassed him," Skye said, not by way of an apology but more with that dreamy motherly tone she had with all her friends.

"We did, but this is far from over. I'm talking to Dallas. He'll agree with me," Sara declared, leaning in to get in Ducky's line of sight. He ignored her as he reached for his headphones. "You're a total transformation dream."

Of course, he heard her but pretended not to as he quickly typed in his complicated password.

"Shoo." Skye waved her hands toward the crowd. "There's nothing else to see," she teased.

Relieved by Skye's intervention, he continued to pay her no attention as he opened his email and focused on the screen. With a tap to the icon, he opened Spotify. He clicked his playlist, drowning out the world and his embarrassment with it.

A surge of energy pumped through Chad like a healing balm against all the doubts plaguing him. The breakneck speed of the wave he rode was nothing compared to the rush of adrenaline jolting through his body, slowing each second that passed down to a crawl. Time felt infinite.

The briny wall of water pushed him forward, the surfboard responding under his feet as he shifted his weight. What a fucking high. Sensory overload in a majestic, soul enhancing way. Far better than any sex he'd ever had. Maybe the best moment of his life.

His thighs and calves burned. Exhilaration rushed through his veins, making his heart hammer in his chest. This was exactly what he needed. The ocean's roar became a tribal anthem in his head. His body acted instinctually, no time for thought to guide his way.

He let his mind go.

Too bad eighteen seconds didn't last a little longer. The wave came to an end, closing out. Chad rode as far as he could before being dumped into the salt water. Without the roar of the wave behind him, he could hear his buddies, both in the water and on the beach, whoop with excitement. The world slammed back into his reality with the same vengeance it had escaped only moments ago.

After a day of wipeouts—many, many failed attempts— Chad let the ocean take him under with a grin etched on his face. His mind blanked of anything more than what a ride that was.

He popped out of the water. The bright sun transformed

the top of the water into blue sparkling crystals for as far as the eye could see. He let himself be hypnotized by the beauty. He dropped back underwater and stretched his body out, swimming the few feet to shore until he could easily stand on the sandy bottom. Damn, if he were going to go pro with any sport, why the hell couldn't it have been surfing?

Chad grinned at the easy answer. Dallas, Texas, his hometown, was landlocked. As a kid, his only chance to surf was at Hurricane Harbor's water park where he had gone to impress the girls with his crazy skill. The ridiculous memory widened his grin as he grabbed his board and trudged toward shore. His buddies met him with all the exuberance that only came from catching the perfect wave after so many failed attempts.

"Bruh, that was sick. That wave was off the hook," Clay, one of Kai's longtime friends, said, reaching out for a congratulatory hand slap with Chad.

"Yeah, I didn't think it was going to happen for me today," Chad said, slogging through the wet sand at his feet.

"Kai said you had it in you," another one of his friends said as he ran up on Chad. "You kicked it up a notch. I almost saw your fins on that turn." These were true compliments coming from a team of guys who had probably surfed seventy percent of their lives. His chest swelled. He did feel like a badass for what he'd just done.

Chad's ass barely had time to hit the sand before Kai caught his next wave, making Chad's ride look like child's play. The surfer knew his way around a wave. Of course, Kai showed up, coming through the wave to hit the lip, executing a perfect three-sixty rodeo flip. His spin was so fast that Kai could have easily done a second one before the board hit the wave again.

The showman didn't end his run there. Kai played the wave like a musician playing an instrument, easily gliding through several well executed turns, creating soaring sprays behind each pivot. Where Chad had let the wave dictate his balance and moves, Kai owned the water, slaying it to his every advantage.

Kai rode the board like a chariot all the way to the shore until he chose to step off. The hoots and hollers from everyone on the beach rivaled that of a local high school football game. Kai's groupie-style following went insane.

Chad found himself wrapped up in it too, although he stayed put, his toes digging into the warm sand. The ebbing adrenaline left him comfortable, content, if not exhausted from the lack of sleep since he'd arrived. He gave his friend one of his loudest whistles, the kind he'd been told pierced a person's brain, before he fell back on the sand, closing his eyes against the bright sun and enjoying the warmth on his skin as he contemplated his choices.

If this was how Kai could perform in his time off, then yes, Tristan needed Kai to headline Wilder Sports, but Chad couldn't imagine what this sponsorship was going to cost his stepfather.

Chad jackknifed up, realizing he hadn't videoed a single moment of the last forty-eight hours. With all these people on the beach, surely someone had. He'd work that out at the bar later tonight where lots of these fans followed Kai's every move.

Chad dropped back on the sand, wondering how he'd ever let life get him down when places like this existed in the world.

CHAPTER 3
FRIENDS

For Ducky, there wasn't much better than the welcoming solitude of his apartment. He kicked the front door closed harder than he'd intended but not near loud enough to provoke his upstairs neighbor to beat her broom against his ceiling, but there it was. His neighbor, an older woman who lived alone, had been up there beating on her floor since he and Dallas had first moved in. He decided the banging must be more greeting than anything else.

"Hi, Mrs. Henson," he called out, louder than the sound of the slamming door, to make sure he was heard.

The knocking came again. She was like the mother hen he'd never really wanted, looking out for him all the time since Dallas had moved out.

He dropped his apartment key on the counter and went for the refrigerator where his chef had left a gourmet meal prepared for him. They were currently trying to bulk him up. His trainer worked alongside his chef to get the right meal ingredients down to help enhance his changing body. A prototype of a program StreamTrainer hoped to add to their list of services next year. Tonight's dinner contained salmon, quinoa, and asparagus in a bowl. Avocado slices and edamame waited to be added. He read the heating instructions and let the quiet of his apartment ease some of the burden of the day.

Work was too busy. Even as he thought the words, the ache in his neck and back caused him to roll his shoulders. As much as he hated to admit it, he probably did need some help—an assistant trained in information technology. Dallas had an assistant, so did Skye. Both worked hard but didn't carry the load Ducky did. Trusting someone to have the company's best interest at heart had been his main issue. But at this point, Ducky couldn't monitor everything by himself.

A knock on the door had Ducky looking in that direction as if he could see who was there. He then glanced at the time, a little past nine. It better not be Greer wanting to get in a quick workout. He'd had to hang up on a jovial Greer and his brother who'd FaceTimed him after hearing about the haircut. He grabbed the bowl, dumped the avocado and edamame inside, and took the utensils, forgoing the warming, and dug in as he went for the door.

Chomping on a big bite from the bowl, he leaned in to look out the peephole. His neighbor stood on the other side, balancing a couple of dishes. With his fork in hand, he opened the door, her glare riveted to his freshly cut hair.

"I didn't think it was you," she said by way of greeting.

"Come in, Mrs. Henson." He stepped back, opening the door wide. She barely budged an inch.

"I'm concerned about you. You're leaving before the sun comes up then coming home so late. I never hear anything down here anymore, and tonight, I thought you were a stranger walking up the stairs." She finally did take a step in long enough to dump clean bowls onto his counter unceremoniously. "And your meals have changed. This isn't all the fast food you used to eat."

"You're concerned about me eating healthy?" he asked with a good-natured chuckle, unsure if she was irritated or concerned. Neither mattered more than adding another bite to his mouth to satisfy his rumbling belly. When he'd started this transformation, he'd asked the chef to drop meals off to his upstairs neighbor too. Not that he knew much about her, they barely spoke over the years, but she was so much like him, alone all the time. Except he wasn't sure hers was by choice. Her tone was always full of piss and vinegar.

"Exactly. It's not the artery clogging food you always eat." She stepped back out the door, her tone dismissive, and started to leave him. "Thank you for sending me the meals."

He added another bite to his mouth and nodded, fighting and failing the grin.

"You also look more like your brother now. It's a good look for you." She never turned back as she headed for the outside stairwell. "I have a granddaughter in Glen Rose if you're lookin'."

That had Ducky's brows lifting. He stepped through the doorway, leaning his ass against the doorframe as he watched her go. Those were probably more words than they had ever spoken before. He watched her until he couldn't see her any longer then waited until he heard her apartment door shut. Dallas was never going to believe their latest exchange.

Weirder, she had offered to set him up with her granddaughter. In all the years he knew her, he had no idea she even had a family.

That was the third time today someone told him he looked like Dallas. Even Greer had made the comment. His brother was the best-looking guy in any room. The only person who didn't agree was Dallas himself. There was no way the compliment could be true, but he liked hearing it. He stepped back inside, shut the door behind him, twisting the locks in place.

He hadn't moved from his and Dallas's apartment mainly due to his aversion to change, but he had decorated the shit out of the place. His bedroom was the same room. Dallas's bedroom had sat empty for a long time just in case he ever wanted to come back. Now that room was his StreamTrainer workout room along with the demo row machine scheduled to launch this fall before the holiday spending season.

It was the living room that was badass. He set the room up with a massive L-shaped desk that held six monitors and his own server. The rest of the room had functional furniture designed to transform from a sitting device to small desks for his team to practice and compete in their tournaments.

The extensive LED lights made the place look showtime game ready. He should think about upgrading his living quarters. His electric bill was insane for all the energy he pulled, running the equipment, and keeping the place at a cool seventy degrees. And maybe he would leave. But this small apartment was easy to maintain.

He dropped down in his gaming chair. The face recognition program brought his monitors to life and lit the LED lights all around the room. He'd disconnected the speech option because he seriously couldn't listen to another person asking him what to do anymore. He looked down at the bowl, knocking around the edamame to mix it with the salmon for the perfect bite.

The heel of his runners hit the edge of the desk as he leaned back in his chair. He shifted the keyboard to his lap, switching it for the bowl. He didn't look at anything work-related and instead decided to text message Chad Reeves to see if he might be up for a League game. Nothing too strenuous, something to take his mind off things. His gaming team took everything so seriously. Ducky recognized the change inside him. Three months ago, he'd have agreed with them that recreational play was useless, but now...

He opened the text app and typed a quick message to Chad, blocking out all the give and take inside his head.

"You around?" Direct and to the point. He hit send and reached for his bowl. He barely got a bite in before the three dots bounced on his screen. He shoveled another bite into his mouth as Chad's reply came through.

"I'm here but in Costa Rica. I can talk. Can't play tho."

Ducky's brows furrowed. He didn't remember Chad mentioning the trip. He absently dropped the bowl on the desk before typing.

"When did you go to Costa Rica? Why?" Ducky waited for Chad's response, staring at the screen. The answers came in rapid-fire succession.

"Tristan's pushing Wilder Sports."

"Kai's surfing here as an interview, I guess that's the best way to explain it."

"I rode a bitchin wave today. Now I'm at a local bar."

"Not really fitting in. I'm told it's hard to shake the Dallas off me."

Ducky started to respond, grinning at such an idea. Chad oozed that same sophistication that Greer had, except different. Chad was a professional athlete and relatable. Class structure didn't matter to him in the least. Ducky hadn't seen Chad in a country club or even out among people, but he bet Chad knew how to get along anywhere.

The phone rang, drawing Ducky from the mental image of Chad's easy, ready smile. The guy preferred to be happy. After living a life under his father's then oldest brother's oppressive anger, Ducky found happiness a very attractive quality. He reached for his headphones and clicked the accept option.

"Hello."

Ducky seemed so grounded and normal. Chad swallowed the last of his ice water and moved off his seat, pointing to his phone. Only the brunette who had glued herself to his side seemed to notice his pending departure. "I've got to take this."

He shoved a finger into his free ear to drown out the noise as he stepped away from his stool, going for the front doors. "Hey. Hang on. I'm going outside."

No matter how hard he tried, he couldn't hear if Ducky responded.

"Reeves, you out?" Kai called, every head between them turned Chad's way.

"No. Maybe. I gotta take this. It's Duck," he said, waving the phone in the air as if that somehow made his words more audible.

"Can you hear me?" he asked Ducky, letting the swinging doors shut behind him. It still took a few steps down the aging front porch before he could hear Ducky's patient voice repeating.

"I can still hear you. And I can hear you now too. Still

hearing you…"

"How 'bout now?" Chad teased, taking several steps away from the building until he plunged his flip-flops into the cool sand. Those were quickly kicked off as he kept going toward the surf beckoning him over. The loud music faded the farther he went. "I came to see Kai. Tristan made him an offer about an hour ago. Kai accepted without even considering a negotiation."

"That was fast." Ducky didn't sound overly impressed.

"Yeah. Faster than I thought. Kai needs a manager. He could've gotten a hell of a lot more out of Tristan," Chad said, staring out at the dark ocean, watching the moon slowly rise.

"I thought you had a golf tournament coming up." Ducky said the word tournament as if testing the accuracy. That had Chad grinning. Their common ground focused only on gaming. Chad didn't understand the world of programming any more than Ducky understood athletics, but they did try for each other. "When did you decide to go to Costa Rica?" Outside of his mother, Ducky was the only other person in the world who knew Chad's struggle with his fathers. Defeat had him dropping down to the sand and crossing his legs. "I thought you were gonna try that golf mental fatigue counseling retreat…the whatever place you said."

"I was…" Chad replied with all the shame of not being able to follow through with his decision. Golfer's burnout was a real thing and had a tight hold on him. So tight he didn't have it in him to sit with a sports counselor to talk golf for any length of time, especially for multiple days.

"You should be here practicing or resting or playing *League of Legends* with me…" Ducky gave a small laugh. "Or whatever else a golfer does to get ready for his next…match."

As if the lack of sleep was just now a problem, Chad let go of a long yawn and drew his knees up, draping an arm around his legs. "I miss the down time where we spent days online playing games together. We used to ditch class to play. Sucks to grow up. But I rode a lit wave today. Probably the best I've ever done. Want to see the pictures?"

"You mean like you surfed? Sure."

Chad put the call on speaker and worked the gallery until he sent a couple of photos then the video the brunette inside took. That was how she'd become attached to the group. A groupie to her core.

Chad rewatched his video, reliving the high of the ride. "You gotta give surfing a try, Duck. It's straight fire. And you've got to come here. The waves are rugged and rough. It just worked for me today. It was my day."

"Cool, cool. You look like Kai out there," Ducky said.

Chad continued to flip through the individual photos. One being from the bar about an hour ago. He'd thought he blended in well enough with the guys. He wore the same style clothing and thought he'd connected with the casual vibe of literally everyone around him, but the pictures told a different story. Chad was the obvious stand-out. Even in beachwear, the city attitude radiated off him. He looked more like a sport's agent—wrinkle-free clothing, perfect hair, groomed facial hair. His watch alone had to cost more than the dive bar they hung out in.

"Yeah, I wish I did. He's something to see in person. He's incredible," Chad answered, closing his gallery, putting those thoughts away. "How long until The Game Awards?"

"I leave next week, but I'm in over my head. The Riot

Games' PR team is going to start working with me tomorrow. I don't know what I was thinking when I accepted their offer." Ducky's stress and anxiety spoke louder than the words he said.

He was a few years older than Ducky. When they were younger, he got why they didn't hang out outside of gaming. They lived thirty minutes away from one another, might as well have been another state away at that age. Now though, it didn't make much sense except Ducky had never opened that door. He was a true loner, lived life on his terms. Ducky's existence was no different now than it was when he had little more than the clothes on his back.

"You know what you were thinking. It's a dream come true for guys like us. It'd be fire if they asked me to present. If you see Fudge from Cloud 9, I want his autograph. Don't forget." Chad wasn't lying in the least. He'd hang that autograph in his condo for the world to see.

"Go back to whatever you were doing. I wanted to see if you could get on and play a game," Ducky said.

"Everybody in the bar's trashed. I'm not drinking. I'll practice in the morning while they're passed out. Tristan's wanting a letter of acceptance signed before I leave. We'll do something extra when Kai signs the official contract in a few weeks. Maybe I can be out of here by early evening tomorrow." A long yawn slipped free.

He wasn't willing to let Ducky end the call. He lived for these unguarded conversations. They were more infrequent these days, but Ducky always eased Chad's worry. Made life a little less stressful. Maybe it was the deep tenor of Ducky's voice or the way he truly seemed to care about Chad's wellbeing. Who was he kidding? Apparently, himself. Boyhood crushes had metamorphosed into adult crushes, he supposed.

"I can talk unless you want to get off and find someone else to play with."

"I'm good. I just finished dinner and reclined back in my chair. What's it look like there tonight?"

Chad lifted his phone and took a picture. It did little to show the magnitude of beauty surrounding him. Instead of sending the dark picture, he described what he saw. "It's ocean for as far as I can see. Where I'm at right now, the water is calm, not the epic waves south of here..." He lost himself in the explanation of the beauty of his surroundings.

The tension drained off him as the healing balm of the night sky, the back-and-forth cadence of the waves, and the connection with his good friend—his best friend—lulled him into a peaceful conversation. One that lasted hours. So long that he missed the closing of the bar and found himself walking back to the motel, the phone still glued to his ear.

CHAPTER 4
DUCKY WHO

Two weeks later

The hustle and bustle of hurried personnel and gamer celebrities, all talking a mile a minute into their headsets and to their entourages, was just about all Ducky could concentrate on as a full-blown panic attack threatened to take him under. His racing heartbeat and the feeling of losing his breath came on way too quickly to control. If he didn't calm down, he was certain to pass smooth out.

"Breathe," Greer hissed directly into Ducky's face, gripping both of Ducky's shoulders, driving him into a darkened corner backstage at The Game Awards show.

"You need to go out there and do this for me," he practically begged Greer. Ducky bent forward, tucking his head as far between his legs as the tight pants would allow, wishing he'd had the forethought to bring a brown paper bag. Why hadn't Dallas thought of that?

He slowly closed his eyes, praying he didn't blackout right

where he stood. Why would he have ever thought he could pull off something like this?

"Stand up. You'll crease your jacket." Based on the closeness of Greer's voice when the command came, Greer had also leaned over. Ducky didn't bother to open his eyes, nor did he do as Greer instructed. He couldn't. All the effort he could muster was to reach for the button on his suit, work it open and let the suit coat hang free.

"I don't know what I was thinking. I can't do this. You go out there and represent us." The rapid-fire words came on a long exhale. He was seriously going to throw up. He hated being social, let alone having to speak in front of an audience. The thought of so many people watching made his stomach roil. Light-colored circles played against the black backdrop of his eyelids. "I'm gonna make a fool out of StreamTrainer."

"Mr. Reigns, there's been a change in plans," a woman said, lifting Ducky's hope that the change included cutting him from the show entirely. Anyone could see he was clearly unable to perform. "We're going to extend your segment to include Ben Schwartz's presentation of the new *Sonic the Hedgehog* movie trailer." The comforting weight of someone's hand flattened against his back, patting gently. "It's better this way. Ben will do all the heavy lifting out there, don't worry. Jim Carey's doing an exclusive remote. Based on how nervous he is, it looks like it all came together perfectly. Very exciting," she said swiftly and succinctly, talking ninety miles an hour in her exuberance. "No one knows it's coming."

"Great," Greer replied just as enthusiastically. Only Ducky knew that Greer had no idea what the *Sonic the Hedgehog* movie franchise meant to the gaming world. He probably had no idea who Sonic was.

At the same time, Ducky shook his head. "Nothing can change. I memorized my lines. I know it'll take exactly twenty-three steps for me to hit my mark. That can't change."

"Duncan, correct?" she asked, bending over to try to look him in the eyes. "The steps don't change. All you have to do is read the new lines from the monitor. There're only slight changes to include Sonic. The feed's speed is based on your reading progress. Ben's a pro. He'll handle everything. It was always planned to be this way, we just had to keep it a secret."

Under normal circumstances, Ducky would be all over anything Sonic related. He'd been a fan of the game and the show all his life. Even Ben Schwartz was a longtime favorite of Ducky's but the anxiety of a script change on top of the panic attack ready to spill over made his flight response double time. Surely there was someone better suited to be on the stage for the length of two presentations.

An old school compact disc was placed in his line of vision. He lifted his head enough to see a grinning Ben Schwartz standing in their small circle. The excitement of a celebrity crush had him gripping the disc being handed to him and rising. "You take this. Put it in the breast pocket of that fancy suit, and when I say trailer, you pull it out and show the audience. I have a joke planned as if the trailer is on that disc then I'm going to take it from you. It's a breakable disc and will snap in two. Like I broke the only copy. You know, like we don't stream things these days." Ben laughed out loud at his joke. His reaction was enough to have Greer and the backstage hand laughing too.

"Easy peasy," Ben added, then clapped his hands

together with a big giant grin still plastered on his face.

"I'm Ben, by the way, and I got you, bro." Ben stuck out his hand in a good-natured greeting as if his plan should solve all Ducky's worry.

Unfortunately, it didn't. The sound of his drumming heartbeat distracted him from immediately returning the handshake.

"I'm Greer Lockhart. This silent guy is Duncan Reigns. He goes by Ducky, and he's nervous," Greer said, opening Ducky's suit coat and placing the CD in his breast pocket. "Ducky, look at me. You've got to calm down."

Dallas came through their small circle with a bottle of water in hand. His laser beam focus zeroed in on Ducky. "They're the StreamTrainer guys," Ben said to Greer, using all the animation he usually had on television, completely missing the dynamic of Dallas swooping in to save the day.

Ben waggled a finger toward Ducky before hooking a thumb Dallas's direction. "I knew I knew you. He's the one from the commercials that makes us all look bad underneath our clothes."

"Here. Take a drink of this." Dallas didn't stop his forward movement until he'd pushed Ducky back several more steps. "Give me a minute with him?" Dallas used the tone he always did to gather Ducky's full attention and it worked as usual. Ducky instantly calmed, looking straight into Dallas's eyes.

"Is he going to be all right?" Ben asked in that same cheery tone. Ducky caught Greer's hesitant nod in his peripheral, but otherwise he stayed silent.

"Have I ever put you in a situation you couldn't handle?" Dallas asked Ducky.

"No. But you know how I—" Ducky replied.

"No." Dallas's finger lifted to Ducky's lips, silencing him from saying anything more. "Listen to me, Ducky. This is your world." His finger circled around their heads, encompassing the venue. "The people out there watching this awards show are your people. This is no different from going live on Twitch, and you do that all the time." Dallas's hand swept toward the entry to the stage. "Now, I want you to go out there with your head held high, hands together tightly and say what you're supposed to say. Own your shit, Duck. Be the man you want to be. The mover of mountains. You're already there. We all see the real you. It's time you did too."

"Dallas, they changed what I'm supposed to say," Ducky said but Dallas's motivational speech did help edge off the anxiety attack. Ducky was beginning to breathe normally again.

"You got this. Trust me." Dallas took Ducky's lapels, his thumbs skimming down the front. "You're not the same guy you used to be. You own a multimillion-dollar company. You're a badass and it shows. Do this to prove to yourself that you're no longer that same misplaced man. You've figured your shit out. It's all any of us ever want out of life and you did it."

"I didn't do it alone. You helped me," Ducky said, staring Dallas straight in the eyes.

"And you helped me," Dallas said forcefully, his stare direct, honest, and strong. "We have each other's backs."

Dallas had been using all these same arguments for months now. Each time Ducky flipped out, Dallas backed him into a corner, asking him to believe in himself. It worked. Ducky finally nodded. The sole reason for all his transformation efforts was to find the inner balance within to help match his outward accomplishments.

He lifted his palms, letting them follow the same trail as Dallas's fingers. Ducky then squared his shoulders and drew in a deep, cleansing breath.

"You're a good brother. You never gave up on me," Ducky whispered, unscrewing the cap to the water bottle.

"There's nothing to give up on."

Ducky seriously doubted that and took one small drink then another. The cool water was precisely what he needed. It gave him the second he needed to regroup and quench his dry throat.

"Schwartz?" a runner called from the edge of the curtain a few feet away. "You and Reigns are on deck."

"Go be brilliant," Dallas said confidently, taking the water bottle with one hand, the other sliding around Ducky's shoulders, turning him toward the stage. "Follow the monitor and keep your hands together. It's all gonna be fine. Don't take it too seriously. Remember every moment while you're out there so you can tell me about it. I'll be here waiting."

Dallas gave him a little shove between the shoulder blades when he didn't readily move forward before Ducky found the courage to take the rest of the steps on his own. This was a life-changing moment… He'd prepared… Not the same scared kid…

He'd never been too sure about his spiritual beliefs, but right then, he decided he believed in everything. Surely if he said a prayer to it all, something had to stick.

The energy in the room vibrated with an excitement that transcended all the worry and bad mood hanging over Chad for the last couple of weeks. Wilder never skimped on any promotion and that included going hard on the new rollout for Wilder Sports. Every minute of the weekend's itinerary was meticulously planned. Full of public relations events designed to entice the full scope of media to follow each step of the way.

Tristan had conceded and done what Chad had requested, using Kai as the first athlete to launch Wilder Sports. It hadn't even been much of an argument, probably due to the overwhelming fact that Chad's performance on tour had left him ranked dead last in the averages. So low that his world ranking average put him at risk of losing his spot in the PGA. He'd once been a bright star, zipping through the ranks. Now his outlook was nothing more than a darkening ember with little hope of recovery. At least, not anytime soon. Sports news was abuzz with his complete failure in the PGA. Woo-freaking-hoo.

Chad didn't let himself dwell, scooting right past that blistering thought. Tristan and Kai signed their respective contracts while on-air live with the brand-new Wilder Sports Podcast.

After Tristan finished signing and tossed the ink pen on the table, a giant grin split his face. He leaned over, taking one of several duffel bags from the floor beside his chair. They were full of the new WS logoed gear for Kai and his entourage that sat around the small room. Tristan tossed each person a full duffel bag.

They were also live streaming the event on the homepage of the Wilder search engine—something they'd never done before in the history of the company. Today, and today only, anytime anyone from around the world searched on Wilder, the screen opened to this live stream. Millions and millions of people were watching Wilder introduce the newest venture added to the many enterprises Tristan owned. A chat feed ran the length of the right side of the screen.

Chad and the group sat side by side at a small, round table. It was compact, but large enough for the six of them. Each had their own microphone. Two laptops sat on the table about a foot away. The overall design was made to look intimate, fresh, and budgeted.

After the signing, Kai, Chad, and the guys were going live on Twitch for a couple of hours to watch The Game Show Awards. Of course, rights and infringements didn't allow Wilder to air the show, all they could do was give commentary, but Tristan had gone over the allotted time with the contracts—the man was never on time. Now they were performing double duty of live streaming on both the show and the contract signing at the same time.

"This is fire," Kai said and started pulling out all the promotional items from the duffle bag. "Blue's my color."

"Chad…" Tristan started then lowered his voice. "Not to put you on the spot…" Tristan chuckled and couldn't hold Chad's direct confused stare as his laughter grew. He slid two blue Wilder Sports embossed folders toward him. They were different style folders than Kai's. Designed for privacy. The move seemed calculated while the others were distracted, yet everything they did was being seen by so many people on the stream.

"You take your time with this one." Tristan patted the top folder. "It's open until you decide what you want to do. You earned this decision. We're here because of you. I just wanted to make it official. If it's an easy one for you, we can broadcast the change today. It's the reason your father isn't with us now."

Tristan lifted a hand, giving a fatherly squeeze to Chad's shoulder as Kai stood, pulling the surfer shirt over his head. Chad ignored all the hoopla and the gazillion hearts rising from the bottom of the screen, and lifted the folder from the bottom edge, blocking anything inside from being seen.

He didn't expect this. Far, far from it.

It wasn't the professional sponsorship he assumed. Instead, he'd been offered the executive role of senior vice president of the newly formed Wilder Sports, Inc. He scanned down the list of responsibilities, which was long and thorough, to the obscenely high salary at the bottom. It took a second to register the seven-figure income, including salary, bonuses, and various other incentives. His heart did a weird twist before his gaze trailed back up the document again, taking a closer look at the responsibilities.

The program was his to be run as he saw fit.

His gaze collided with Tristan's who then busted out with a genuine laugh which Chad took to mean he must look as stunned and blindsided as he felt. "You earned it. This weekend's yours."

"Dude, Ducky's on." Kai knocked Chad in the chest as he toppled back down into his seat to watch their friend. The three of them—Kai, Ducky, and Chad—had originally met on Twitch years ago while playing *League of Legends* together.

Ducky. Probably the only thing that could have made Chad turn away from the astounding offer Tristan surprised him with. His gaze riveted to Ducky. Everything in the room faded as Ducky grinned at something Ben Schwartz said to the audience. The smile was genuine, sincere, and one of Ducky's most captivating qualities.

Ducky's smile held Chad transfixed for a split second before a ton of bricks landed on his chest, his brain finally catching up to what he was seeing. The weight of the conflicting emotions brought him to his knees—figuratively speaking. The sound of blood rushing through his veins to supply his galloping heart deafened Ducky's words. The edge of his peripheral vision dimmed. His focus locked on the gorgeous man on screen. The world narrowed to only him and Ducky. His primal instincts flipped the fuck out.

His cock punched against his cargo shorts, demanding to be set free. Heat flooded his face and spread through his body like wildfire. The man of his dreams had transformed into the man of his wet dreams. Motherfucker. What the hell had happened to Ducky?

When did that happened? He was stunning. Ducky looked like a hotter version of his older brother. Who knew that handsome face lurked under all that hair?

Ducky cut his hair… A defensive side leapt to the forefront, causing Chad's brow to crease. A protectiveness exclusive to Ducky had him resisting his own reaction.

Ducky was perfect the way he was. Who had made him do this?

"What happened to Ducky?" Chad murmured quietly, shaking his head, wishing Ducky knew that Chad had always thought he was beautiful the way he was.

Truth be known, Chad always had a massive weak spot for the wild curls.

Chad's mouth went dry as he scanned the tailor-made suit, Ducky's strong jawline, and that familiar smile he could lose himself in over and over again. The long curls had been cut and styled into perfect thick waves that Chad had the sudden urge to run his fingers through.

No one could deny Ducky looked damn good this way too.

The pressure of a hand on his back, coupled with the need for an emotional break drew Chad back into the moment. He heaved a sigh, again wondering when Ducky had made such a change. Kai and his crew had crowded together to get a better look at Ducky's transformation. Chad could see by the Twitch feed that there were equal parts excitement about the new Sonic movie and Ducky's new look. No one must have known about these changes. It had been a surprise to the viewers too.

"Are you good?" Tristan asked quietly.

Chad glanced over at his concerned stepfather who had clearly witnessed Chad's hard visceral reaction to Ducky. A truth Chad had never shared with his father or Tristan before. The rawness of emotion had Chad lifting a hand toward the screen. "I don't think… That's not Ducky. What happened to him?"

Tristan turned toward the laptop before his confused gaze flipped back to Chad as if questioning his sanity. Luckily, Kai's over-the-top personality took the room and Tristan's attention, giving Chad a moment to recover. He sat back in his seat, bringing the ice-cold water bottle with him. He chugged long swallows.

What had Ducky done to himself? After hours on the phone, both speaking and texting, why the hell hadn't he told him about the changes? Given Chad some sort of heads up? That wasn't cool at all. He swiped a damp, clammy hand over his face, praying that the strain in his shorts would end soon. He never knew for sure where Ducky was concerned.

CHAPTER 5
SHOWTIME

The bright lights and competing sounds coming from every direction drowned out everything else, even the drumming in Ducky's ears as he stood on stage, staring at Jim Carey's video. His fingers hurt from the death grip he held them fisted in while tucked in his pants pockets. A last second adjustment he made while walking out on the stage, maybe better than holding his hands so tightly in front of his jacket for the world to see, but otherwise, it worked just like Dallas said. He wasn't fidgeting and he didn't think he had embarrassed himself or StreamTrainer too badly. They'd been right: Ben handled everything. Even making a show of helping Ducky read his first lines to the laughter of both the crowd and Ducky himself.

Ben's elbow knocked him in the arm. "You were fire out there."

Ducky only rolled his eyes and gave an almost nonexistent shake of the head. "Kindling maybe."

It took a second for Ben to get his joke before looking at

him and busting out with uncontrolled laughter. "There you go, buddy. I knew you had it in you."

Normally, when someone gave Ducky a good-natured whack on the back, he'd be sent stumbling forward a step or two. But not this time. He was stronger now. More muscular. That made him feel good too.

The video ended, the screen darkened, and in unison, they turned back toward the audience where he could literally see nothing past the bright spotlights. Ben ended their segment to a rousing applause to Sonic which was damn cool to Ducky.

Finally, the coolness of the moment settled in. The seven or eight seconds of walking off the stage were about the best moments of his life to date. He took in the fragrance of the air. How did they know exactly what gaming smelled like?

All that anxiety for nothing. Just like the entire journey, from being given the opportunity to present an award today, to transforming his body and appearance so he didn't embarrass himself too badly, to actually being on this stage, it all fell into a good place.

Ducky was his own problem, always getting in his way of adapting and managing life.

Wow. What a revelation.

Ducky's relief flooded out in the form of a grin when he saw Dallas and Greer waiting in the distance then heading his way. The rush and clamor of the backstage pandemonium no longer involved him. He had to shuffle a few steps to get out of the way of the new presenters while shrugging out of the tight fit of the suit coat. The thing about these glove-like fitting clothes was that they wore like a second skin. They had no give. He could always feel them on his body.

Getting out of these clothes seemed the only thing he could concentrate on and immediately started to work the silk tie from his neck. Ben whacked him on the back again, this time catching him off guard, knocking him forward a step. What was with all this back whacking stuff?

"See ya round, bud. Send me one of the boxes everybody's talking about." Ben winked at Ducky. He had that charismatic thing down that Ducky wished he had. A personality that easily put a smile on people's faces. Not the quizzical looks Ducky usually got when he tried to be charming. Maybe that was what he needed to work on next. It seemed insurmountable.

"You did it. How do you feel?" Greer asked, drawing him into a hug. Dallas was right there beside him. Ducky was lost in all the goodness of the moment, and his hands were crunched between him and Greer as he got the fatherly bearhug.

"It was good. All that freak out was for nothing," he admitted, his finger still loosening the single tie knot as he stared up at the darkened rafters in the ceiling. Ducky was the same height as Greer but had to cast his glance up to look at Dallas. They shared so many of the same features. The same whiskey-colored eyes sparkled with happiness— something new for the both of them.

"You're right, for nothing," Dallas agreed. Ducky nodded, a confirming single nod as Greer let him go, allowing him room to release the small button at his neck. It seemed the first real breath he'd had since dressing that morning.

"Hey. You gotta look the part all the time," Greer said, eyeing the way Ducky was disrobing, wrapping an arm around Ducky's shoulders. "Never break. You'll get used to it."

"My plan's to remove this shirt and turn my T-shirt inside out, or right side out, whichever. I like your clothes, Greer, but I think I like 'em better on you."

Dallas barked out a laugh as they started for the exit.

"There's a dumpling place not far from here that I heard the staff talking about," Dallas said, catching the side exit door and pushing it open for Ducky to walk out first. "Let's get something to eat while my little brother, the celebrity, tells us what it was like."

"Plan," Ducky said and followed through with his threat, pulling his shirt tails free. The weight of the world lifted, and in its place slid relief. The months he'd prepared for this moment weren't for nothing. He'd done it. "Here. Hold these."

Ducky handed Dallas his suit coat, dress shirt, and silk tie as Greer went to the curb to hail a cab. Ducky pulled the T-shirt over his head, quickly changing sides.

"Come on. I got a cab," Greer said from the curb then dropped his hand, turning back to Ducky with shocked outrage. "Ducky! What are you doing?"

That question blanketed so many possible topics, and Ducky didn't care to answer any of them. He'd gotten a good dose of sophisticated clothing, which in his opinion bordered on torture. The clothes were too claustrophobic for him. He needed a style that fit somewhere in the middle because the thought of wearing these clothes all the time sent a shiver down his spine. He went for the cab, pulling the T-shirt down his body.

"I believe I'm the celebrity so that makes you my entourage, not my mentor." Ducky barely got the joke out before sliding into the backseat of the cab. Greer's mouth dropped open, rendering him speechless, causing Ducky and Dallas both to laugh hilariously. Greer was never at a loss for words.

Chad could feel the deep etch of the frown on his face. They were still in the middle of the live stream. His reaction to Ducky and the award show or, maybe better said, the lack of a reaction was being witnessed by the millions of people tuned in, but he doubted anyone paid attention to him with such a hottie like Ducky on the screen.

He needed to gather himself. Get a hold of all these resurfacing desires he thought he'd processed and dealt with years ago. The only way to get that time was by leaving the room, taking a few minutes to himself. Yet, his ass remained planted in the seat, his gaze riveted to the small screen, held utterly captivated by the Twitch commentary and replay clips of Ducky and the new *Sonic the Hedgehog* movie trailer.

The shock of Ducky's transformation slowly morphed into fascination. Ducky was the most authentic person he had ever known. The friend who grounded Chad the most. Who made him feel normal and whole and was now grinning on a stage in front of millions of people as if he owned that audience. Ducky lit up the stage with his presence and stood in such a way that he exuded confidence, as if he did these kinds of things all the time.

Did he not know Ducky at all?

Chad raced through his memories, replaying the nervousness in Ducky's voice when he spoke about the upcoming show. He never hinted at any of these changes in his appearance. Chad tucked his hands in his cargo shorts, hoping to make extra room to hide his rigid hard-on. He let himself get lost in what he was seeing. Ducky was gorgeous. Truly handsome. He suspected there was muscle growth under the tight-fitting suit.

Yeah, apparently, he hadn't reconciled any of the longing he'd had for Ducky all these years. Now there was a new version for Chad to lose his shit over. Not a better model, just another side to Ducky's enormous depth.

As the commentary came to an end, and Ducky disappeared from the screen, the message board zipped up the side in lightning speed. Chad didn't engage. He needed to take an emotional step back. He rose from his seat and shoved the chair underneath the table, trying to keep the obvious reaction in his shorts unseen. "I'm going to the bathroom."

"Yeah, I got this." Kai's hand came out, slapping Chad's. "Our boy gave us a curve. He was extra tho."

"Like fire," Chad responded, sounding lame, and pointed to the message boards. "He's calling to do a remote with us soon. I'll be back."

Like the coward he'd become, Chad ignored Tristan completely, giving him his back as he started out of the room. Tristan wasn't to be put off. He followed Chad out into the hall. Several members of the production team littered the hallway. Wires ran from outlets all the way down the long walkway, causing Chad to focus on where he stepped to keep from tripping and falling.

"Hey," Tristan called out, which only caused Chad to hurry his steps. It wasn't inconceivable that Tristan could have spoken to anyone else in the hall, but he tried his best to ignore him. "Give me a minute, son."

Son. Chad rolled his eyes and kept going. No way they were having this conversation for everyone in Wilder to hear.

"You're the only one who gets away with ignoring the CEO of our company," Landry, Tristan's number two man said, chuckling at Chad as he walked past. "Apparently, he's gotta pee real bad, Tristan."

"Give me a minute, Landry," Tristan replied, not to be distracted.

His serious tone caused Chad to stop in the middle of pushing open the bathroom door, his shoulders tightening. He lowered his head and kept going to look under the stalls, making sure they were completely alone. He had seconds to form his thoughts and a strategy.

He could say he'd never had a reaction like that before, but Tristan would call him on his bullshit.

The door swung open, and Chad twisted around, startled as if he hadn't expected Tristan to be there. The Ducky-induced arousal faded. Not only faded, but his balls shrunk until they may have been reabsorbed into his body. Tristan came directly to him, forcing Chad to hold his ground when all he wanted to do was retreat.

His stepfather gripped his shoulders with the same amount of sweet-but-firm hold as before and said, "You have nothing to worry about with me. You can say, do, or be whoever you are and it's good with me. You have to know that."

Of course Chad knew but it didn't stop a deeply held exhale from escaping his lungs. Chad rolled his eyes and gently slipped from the hold. He scrubbed his hands down his face.

He was having an existential crisis with every part of his

pathetic life. He had the hots for one of his best friends, a friend, mind you, who had only ever talked about women. For some reason, he didn't want to play golf anymore. It had been his journey for the last many years. He'd fought his family to even finish college. He lived, ate, breathed golf, and now he just didn't want to do it.

Jesus. He was losing his fucking mind.

Instead of letting the crazy out for Tristan to see, Chad scraped his fingers through his hair and said the exact opposite of what he felt. "You don't think I can handle the pros. I get it, Tristan. You don't have to explain anything else." Chad swung around, going to the sink to splash cold water on his face.

He needed to get into some counseling.

No, he needed a lobotomy.

All he seemed to want in the world was to have Ducky standing here with him, holding his hand, helping him navigate these changes.

No, that wasn't true. He wanted Ducky in that stall, pumping his cock in and out of Chad's mouth.

No. No. Not a thought to have right now, you ass.

He wondered what the shape of Ducky's ass looked like now. Chad's entire body hardened under the cold splash of water on his cheeks.

"You want my honest answer to what you just said?" Patient sincerity dripped from Tristan's tone as he handed Chad a wad of paper towels to dry himself off. "I don't think you really want what you're striving for."

How the hell did Tristan do that? Cut straight through Chad's bullshit like that? "What?" Chad asked and stopped in the middle of wiping the towels over his face. Their gazes connected in the mirror above the sink. "I've worked damned hard…"

Tristan lifted one hand, stopping him from digging himself further into the hole of lies he created. "I've watched you for years. You conquered college with a vengeance, earning a master's degree in the same time it takes most people to graduate with their undergrad. You laser-focused on professional golf. I've never seen anyone work as hard as you've worked to get where you are. It's almost as if you're running from something." Tristan said the words then let them sit there between them as he turned toward the bathroom door to leave. "I'm always here for you. I won't push you, Chad, but I promise you won't find balance until you become comfortable with who you are. Do I say anything to your dad about this?"

"No, not yet," Chad said instantly. All his bullshit and diversion was only to try to throw Tristan off track to keep from telling his dad what had happened. His father worried too much about his kids and how his life change had affected them.

Another layer of guilt sat heavily in his gut.

Tristan nodded and stepped out of the room. The door shut, closing him alone in the space. Chad didn't waste another minute. He tossed the towels in the trash, patting his pockets for his cell phone. He had to let Ducky know he'd taken him by surprise and how amazing he looked. What a great job he'd done presenting. But he didn't have his phone.

Shit, he'd left it on the table. God dammit. It would have to wait.

Chad stared at himself in the mirror.

His whole body stilled as he blinked at his reflection. Ducky Reigns was a straight-up hottie.

Since his youth, he'd managed his attraction for Ducky by assuming he had time to make things happen between them—if anything was going to happen between them. If Ducky was even gay, bisexual, or interested in building something more between them. That strategy had helped stave off the intensity of all the wanting he'd done for as long as he could remember. This new development threatened everything.

CHAPTER 6
CANCELED

"I wanted to drop in and say hey, I can't be on too long," Ducky said to Kai from the Twitch app on his phone while crammed inside the backseat of the cab, sandwiched between Dallas and Greer. He used to fit better than he did these days.

"I should have gotten us a car," Greer whispered. He didn't live in the live stream world and probably believed he couldn't be heard.

"It's a surprise you didn't," Dallas said in the same hushed tone, making Ducky laugh as Dallas struggled to make more room for his brawny muscles, finally throwing an arm behind Ducky's back, pushing him forward.

He turned the phone's screen first in Greer's direction, who grinned that charming smile he had and lifted two fingers in a peace sign.

"That's Greer Lockhart, my brother-in-law. And this is Dallas. You guys know him. He's my brother. We own StreamTrainer together."

"Dude, that was sick. You have so much explaining to do. Reeves thought you were capping, that it wasn't actually you," Kai said, his face filling the screen. "You changed your whole look. Who knew there was a decent face under all that hair?"

The relief of being done, coupled with the feeling of actually hearing all his hard work had paid off, had a giggle welling inside him. In his wildest dreams, he'd never anticipated his makeover reveal going so well. "Two eyes, a nose, and a mouth."

"And we can see 'em now, bro," Johnnie-boy, Kai's best buddy, interjected, pushing Kai out of the way to get in the camera's range. "And what's up presenting Sonic. Sonic! With Ben freaking Schwartz. You just kept all sorts of secrets."

"That was sprung on me the last few seconds before we went on stage. I was as surprised as you. My cab's stopping," Ducky said, almost toppling over when Dallas opened his door and stepped out. "I gotta go. Did you sign, Kai?"

Kai lifted the logoed hat off his head. "I did. Got some lit merch. We currently have two million viewers on the live stream. That's sick."

"100 Thieves tweeted out a selfie of Matt Haag with you in the distance, bent over with your head between your legs," Johnnie-boy added, bringing his phone closer to the laptop for Ducky to see the tweet.

Ducky bent in, his face filling the entire screen to take a closer look as he stepped out of the cab, directly into oncoming foot traffic. He got knocked in the shoulder one way, sending him into the line of walkers going the other way. He was struck there too. He didn't even care. Too many of his heroes were on him today.

"No way. Matt Haag." He quickly screenshotted the pictures as if he couldn't find the tweet later. Before he was struck again, Dallas gripped the back of his T-shirt and tugged him in the direction of the dumpling house.

"You have to wear the jacket inside," Greer said, holding the door with one hand and the suit coat with the other. In a sea of changes, these two men looking out for him and his scattered ways meant nothing had really changed at all. Even that made him over-the-top happy today.

"I've gotta go. I'll sign on later. Where's Chad?"

"Seriously, bruh," Kai said. "He didn't believe it was you. You didn't let any of us know."

Ducky nodded and didn't say more. He generally kept his private life private. Had this not worked out, he didn't want to hear the ribbing later.

"Chad'll be back soon. The message board thinks he got pissy about it. He thought they had the wrong presenter when they announced you."

Ducky stopped in mid shrug of pulling the jacket back on. Dallas had to scoot him aside to get inside the restaurant. The loud diners made it hard to hear or be heard, but Ducky became lost in thought of Chad not believing it was him. Every workout, all the clean food, even the hairstyle was done with Chad in the back of his mind.

Chad always looked effortlessly good. Like a male model every single day.

Had Chad hurt his feelings?

"Omigod, is that a pout?" Johnnie-boy asked.

"Yo, I think Ducky's tilted," Kai chimed in, interpreting his confusion as anger.

"I gotta go. They're calling me." Ducky decided there had to be more to the story. Chad wasn't the kind of guy to go hard at anyone's expense except for his sister, Chloe.

"Hey, Reeves is back," Kai blurted a second before Ducky touched a finger to the screen to disconnect the call.

He'd figure it all out later. Right now, he was going to eat the first real food he'd had in a month.

He finished shrugging on his suit coat and looked around for Dallas. He stood close to a table where Greer sat, guiding him over with a wave of the arm.

"I think I want one of those Singapore Slings," Ducky said, taking the seat across from Greer.

"You earned a double," Dallas said, sliding in next to Greer.

"I damn sure did." He reached his hand across the table for a quick knuckle touch. They all earned this carb-filled dinner.

Darkness and dread filled the space around Chad as he scrolled down the feed from their live event earlier in the day. It was the middle of the night, and he was up, wide awake, wondering how things had gotten so out of control. Talk about the power of being canceled in the same amount of time it took to snap a finger. He wasn't sure most of these people even knew what he had said to cause such a ruckus, or if they knew who Ducky was, but his simple comment during a moment of surprise had morphed into an ugly monster, growing legs, feet, arms, two heads and a tail…all on its own.

If this feed was any indicator, Chad had been charged, tried, convicted, and sentenced for his heinous crimes against humanity. He was what was wrong with the world today and needed to be erased from any future narrative about Ducky—whatever that meant.

The Wilder public relations department was in hard problem-solving mode, working on Chad's behalf, trying to repair his accidental blunder. Had they only live streamed on Twitch, it might not have been so bad but because they'd been public on Wilder's search engine, his gaffe had blown up like an atomic bomb.

He swiped up the phone screen and leaned his ass against the edge of his father's kitchen counter where he stayed any time he came to California. Who knew how long he stood there reading the comments on the now trending hashtags #ChadWilderhastogo and #IstandwithDucky. His heart sank and his stomach roiled.

He hadn't meant to imply The Game Awards were trying to pull one over on their audience when he said that wasn't Ducky on stage or that Ducky couldn't have pulled off such a good performance, or good looks, or whatever they accused him of. He'd just been surprised. Stunned. Truth be told he'd been sexually bowled over. He'd never been so attracted to anyone in his life. Not in his entire life, and Ducky had set that bar damn high already.

Why was he explaining this to himself again? He needed Ducky to know.

Except Ducky had gone radio silent. Chad left the feed and went to text messages. He'd sent six messages, the first three were immediately after he walked back into the event room to find he'd missed Ducky's call. The last three were to explain why he said what he said. By explain, he didn't tell the whole truth about being so sexually charged by Ducky. Just that he'd been surprised. He'd hoped to stress there was nothing sinister or nefarious intended.

Ducky had always responded before, so why hadn't he now?

Chad shut off his phone and tossed it on the counter behind him, plunging the room into complete darkness. A yawn built enough to slip out, and he scrubbed his palms down his face in frustration.

He reached for the refrigerator door, needing a can of water, wondering if there was any chance for sleep tonight. His fingertips brushed against something soft, startling the shit out of him. He recoiled his arm away, almost losing his balance as he tried to get away.

"I wasn't quiet," his dad said, amusement in his voice.

Chad's heart thundered against his ribcage as he dropped his head between his shoulder blades, absorbing the scare. "I was distracted. You scared me."

The way his father chuckled made him doubt the plan to scare wasn't somewhere in the mix. The refrigerator door opened, and the light filtered into the dark kitchen.

"A water?" Dylan asked.

"Yeah."

"Can't sleep?"

"Nah," he said and decided to leave it right there. He took the offered water.

"The coverage still got you down?"

Chad rested back against the counter, now across from his father, and flipped the top, taking a long drink as his eyes adjusted to the darkness. People told him all the time that he and his father were cut from the same cloth. Moments like these were where he saw the similarities. Same height, same body build. Chad was lucky his dad had taught him the wonders of athletics. And the bedhead. The thick dark tresses stood on end just like his.

He cut his gaze to the side, out the floor-to-ceiling glass panels. "Why are you up?"

"I'm going for a jog. Wanna join me?" his dad asked. Chad's gaze shifted to the clock on the microwave. How was it already five o'clock in the morning? He hadn't slept all night.

"Yeah, I guess," he said, taking another long drink. A long run was probably the best way to clear his head. "Give me a minute to change."

He pushed off the counter and grabbed his phone, weighing the idea of texting Ducky again. It seemed stalkerish. He'd give it until lunchtime and reevaluate.

CHAPTER 7
THIRST TWEETS

Three days later

Ducky sat on a barstool in the middle of one of StreamTrainer's training studios, caught in the snare of an unexpected media frenzy. Somehow, he found himself in a constant loop of interviews from anyone and everyone with a podcast or social media platform—which was technically their company's target marketing demographic. No outlet was too small, a policy Ducky had initiated years ago when they'd first started to make it big. They always needed to remember how hard they worked to get people to pay attention to their small new business.

The last few days were a tiring blur. The unforgiving schedule pushed him past his mental hang-ups of being shy and reserved. Exhaustion had a way of tamping out those lifelong insecurities. Frustration probably came in a close second with the amount of actual work he was having to field between each interview. Apparently, fatigue and annoyance came off as charming and approachable if the in-real-time focus group studying his performance was to be believed.

None of it made any sense. For most of his life, Ducky enjoyed the title of outcast. He struggled to make any genuine connections with anyone. How had it all changed so quickly?

In the realm of possibility, the one option that made the most sense was that Sara, their PR person, had made it all up to keep him performing as she wanted.

Dallas did that to him all the time.

Whatever. It worked well enough.

In the moments between the chaos, Sara had created an entire advertising campaign, highlighting his physical transformation. A complete before, during, and after. How she'd done it so fast, he had no idea, but man, did she want to push the *go* button. Hell, their entire executive team, excluding Ducky of course, wanted the ads to go live as their first coast-to-coast nationwide campaign.

They nudged at him hard to give in. To see the importance of riding on the wave of all this media buzz created after The Game Awards and after Chad's and Kai's podcast on Wilder.

Ducky narrowed his eyes as he sat contemplating Chad or Kai's possible involvement. Dallas or Greer could have gotten to Chad or Kai first, suggesting Chad say he didn't believe it was truly Ducky on stage. The conspiracy theories ran wild inside his head. Could they have staged the whole thing in hopes of getting this exact response from the media? Chad more than anyone knew how social media worked. His father helped lay the groundwork for the online social revolution.

Pretty clever of those guys. If so, it worked like a charm. The world had turned out in Ducky's defense. Chad wouldn't give a care if he'd been painted as the bad guy. He probably hadn't thought twice about it.

"Ducky, this is Emma with Buzzfeed Celebrity," Sara said. Ducky nodded to the woman on the other side of the monitor in front of him. Their studio's makeup team came forward to lift his hair, straighten his shirt, and do all the things he didn't like at all. Mainly due to his aversion to being touched. "In this segment, you'll read tweets that Buzzfeed has found about you and react to them. The funnier or sillier your response, the better. I'll sit off camera and react with you. Look at me if something throws you off. This'll take about fifteen minutes. Got it?"

He took a deep breath to steady himself. So many questions ran through his crowded mind. Like when did he ever tried to be funny before a day in his life? How could he be funny when he'd slept a total of six hours in four days? Instead of voicing any of that out loud, he put a practiced grin on his face and nodded, sitting a bit straighter in his seat.

Sara turned toward the filming crew, one of his longtime friends behind the camera gave a thumbs up. "Emma is about to start. What you're to say and the tweets you'll read will replace her on the screen." She pointed again to the only monitor in the room.

He rolled his shoulders and nodded before swatting at the hands still touching him. "Let's get this done then take a break. I'm starving."

"Only a fifteen-minute break. Your afternoon schedule is packed," Sara said, shooing everyone off stage. "And at six thirty, you're taking a class with Skye."

"You ready, Ducky?" Emma asked.

Beat down, he didn't say a word about the undiscussed training class and only nodded again. Skye, a part owner in StreamTrainer, worked out their elite users. She kicked everyone's ass. She'd absolutely go harder on him just to make for a better class.

"Four, three…"

The fake smile on his face dimmed as the script appeared on the screen. On the silent count of one, he started to read aloud.

"I'm Duncan Reigns, everyone calls me Ducky, and I'm here with Buzzfeed to read some thirst tweets…" His gaze skidded to Sara. What the hell? Sexy tweets about him? The anxiety he thought he'd conquered rushed forward. His cheeks warmed as he looked directly into the camera and ad-libbed. "You guys are gonna have to wish me luck on this one. Jeez."

"Chad…" His mother, Teri Reeves, said from across her kitchen table. The tone she used spoke of her growing impatience.

He knew every inch of this kitchen by heart. They had spent more time in this room, talking as a family, than in any other room inside his childhood home.

His thoughts were so lost that he didn't immediately look at her. It wasn't that he didn't hear her frustration, he did. He always heard everything she said. For whatever reason, his mother was the guiding voice inside his head, whether he liked it or not. But while in the internal throes of the pity party of his life, this despondent approach had become his new norm.

"Darling, if we're going to have lunch, then let's have lunch." She spoke in the motherly tone of utter patience when she really had none. "If you're going to fiddle with your great-grandmother's figurines, then I'm going to call this done and get back to work." She folded her napkin and placed it on the table beside her plate but didn't budge from her seat.

She was bluffing. They both knew it.

What she did have was a tight schedule. She'd been generous with her time today, fitting him in for a quick lunch. But if he kept dawdling like this, what held the most risk to him was getting wrangled into picking up Cara, his littlest half sister, from elementary school. He fought the shiver racing up his spine at the horror of that awful school pickup line.

That reminder motivated him enough to finally head in the direction of the kitchen table. His mother had prepared her favorite lunch meal and what she believed to be his favorite too. Tuna salad. Her recipe had bite-size pieces of fruit mixed with Miracle Whip—her secret ingredient. One that Chad could do without.

"You're being a sad sack, my favorite son. And you have been for several days now. You're bringing my mood down."

He ignored everything but the obvious and playfully glared at her. "I'm your only son, Mom."

The tease worked as her napkin went to her lap again. She reached for her fork and took a big bite of the salad. "Mmm…"

He took his seat, and did the same, taking a hearty bite. He reached for the mango-flavored unsweet iced tea.

"Cate told me you're the most hated villain on social media these days. You know that's not the real world, right?" she said and lifted her eyes, staring directly at him before taking another bite. That was the thing about having parents who pioneered the development of social media, he'd always been taught to keep the viral world at a distance.

Now that Secret by Wilder had been dragged into the mess he'd caused, Chad wondered if all the negative press might now matter more. It didn't. Not to anyone in their family, including Tristan. Social media was a make-believe land. A place that didn't really exist or hold true merit. Designed only to keep up with family and friends.

"I remember, Mom." Chad placed the fork down, his stomach turning at the idea of eating more food. All the engrained manners his mother instilled into him as a child rose to the surface, at least while he was inside her home. He lifted the napkin to his lips as he got to his feet again, needing the movement.

His appetite had gone to shit. He was losing weight and quite possibly losing his mind. A restlessness coursed through his veins. Teri took the bite on her fork with her gaze following him as he moved. "I don't think the world could hate me more than I hate myself. What's happening to me, Mom?"

She chewed quickly. Alarm replaced the patience she usually held while dealing with him.

"Wait. That was dramatic. I didn't literally mean I hate myself so get that look off your face. I'm fine, I guess." The explanation didn't come as easy as all the self-loathing. He went back to the chair, pulling it out farther from the table and plopping down in the seat. He propped his elbows on his knees. His head hung as he stared at the tiled floor. "I don't want to golf anymore."

Saying it out loud had him lifting his back against the seat, feeling like an utter failure. Who spent years working on their goals only to abandon them to the wind?

"Is that all?" she asked, incredulously.

"Isn't that enough?" Chad asked at the ridiculousness of her question. He propelled himself out of the chair, pacing the length of the small space. "I've been golfing since I was four years old. It's been my whole life since I graduated from college. Y'all dumped so much money into my success so I could follow my dreams."

"And you did follow your dream, dear. And you've paid us back some pretend number you came up with in your head when we insisted you didn't have to. Chad, you did it. You reached your goals. You always do. You're unstoppable when something gets inside your head." Classic Mom. She had a way of easily seeing all the angles to tie them up in a pretty little motivational, supporting bow.

He bet that pissed her counterparts off in the courtroom. It grated on his nerves right now, and she was literally his closest friend.

"You've always set almost impossible goals for yourself. You work hard to reach the outcome you want then move on. It's how you've always been since you were a little boy. Remember those cliff divers at the river? We were horrified when you ran headfirst, full steam ahead, and flung your little body off the side of the cliff."

Of course, he didn't remember. That happened twenty years ago. He was five years old. The stunt resulted in a broken arm and a goose egg the size of a kiwi on his head, or so the story went. His father had run after him, diving straight into the water, most likely saving Chad's life. That part of the story was etched into his memory.

"But that's not all that's bothering you, is it?" she asked, continuing to read him like a book, getting to the real reason he'd come by today. "Is it Tristan's offer?"

What? He threw his hands in the air. Of course, she knew about the offer. Their small family was like a small town. They all knew each other's secrets. The whole reason he kept his private matters so close to his chest.

"No…" Chad hedged. What did it say about him that he hadn't even considered such a significant offer since it had been given?

That alone showed how fucked in the head he was.

"Do you want me to continue to guess?" she asked. "Those trousers don't really match the cut of your sweater. Do we need to go shopping? Is that it?"

Her silliness fell over him like a ton of bricks. "Mom. Don't trivialize this. I think I need serious counseling. Maybe a mental health inpatient stay somewhere. I'm a wreck. It's…"

His mom's throaty chuckle drew Chad's frustrated gaze toward her. If she planned to laugh at him, he could go talk to one of his sisters about his problems. Chloe, in fact. She never gave him a break on anything.

"Babe, I have lived with Reeves men for most of my adult life. I raised children with one. Your grandmother, your nana, has told me things about her experience with your grandfather. I promise, whatever is happening to you is within your ability to control." She lifted her fork again, preparing another bite as if that bit of advice solved everything. "You only have to be willing to face your problem head on. Reeves men aren't cowards. Deal with it."

She took her bite as she winked at him.

What did that even mean?

Maybe he'd been wrong to come here.

"Mom, I gotta go," Chad finally said, digging in his pocket for his key fob. Besides, these pleated khakis went with everything. What was she even talking about? "This is serious for me. I'll call you in a few days."

His mom rose from her seat, going around the table as she came for him. "Let me finish. There's no one steadier than a Reeves man when he knows himself and knows what he wants." She reached for his cheeks, keeping him close, staring him directly in the eyes. "Are you drinking too much?"

Whatever she saw on his face made her step back and cross her arms over her chest, contemplating him. She didn't shy away from the direct question and continued to stare him straight in the eyes, waiting for an answer. The question came from a place of love. His father had a problem with alcohol. Something Chad, Chloe, and Cate watched for in themselves.

Chad let go of an unsteady breath. The rawness of exposure made him cross his arms tightly over his chest, holding himself together. "No, not really. I only have one or two, here and there. Drinking isn't the problem."

She nodded. Compassion hinted in her serious expression. "Then who is he?" she asked as if it were a given next option.

Hell, maybe it was. She had lived with his father for eighteen years, knowing he was gay for most of that time.

Technically, her question should have made this easier on Chad, but it didn't. With all the mean-spirited harassment he'd received from the kids in his high school when his father came out, and the untold amount of bullshit he'd had to deal with when their private family affairs began to be splattered all over the local news, made talking about a long-term relationship with another man anything but casual…

Whoa. Step way *back.*

Wait a damn minute. Long-term relationship? That thought had struck him like a blow from out of nowhere.

Wow, what a moment for an epiphany. He ran unsteady hands nervously through his hair. A long-term commitment from Ducky? Is that what he wanted?

Ducky had never given him any clue that he was anything other than a straight man. Not any of those telltale signs indicating interest in the same sex. The bigger problem was that Ducky hadn't spoken to him in days. Not one word to all of Chad's texts apologizing for his unguarded comment.

His heart dipped then fluttered, sending a shiver from his head to his toes and racing back up his spine again. He didn't like Ducky ignoring him, not one bit. Anyone but Ducky.

"Ducky," he finally whispered. Funny how saying the name out loud seemed to validate his feelings, giving him an inner boost.

His mother blinked then opened her mouth to speak. No words came as she blinked again, closing her mouth. Her head tilted quizzically, and her hand lifted about six inches from her head. She shook her fingers. He took it to indicate Ducky's mop of curls.

First smile in days. "Yes. Except he's changed, but I was really into those curls."

Chad reached for the cell phone in his back pocket, bringing up an image of Ducky that he'd saved from The Game Awards. He turned the screen to show his mother Ducky's new look.

She pretty much had the same reaction he had. A

moment of pure confusion as she stared at the screen before she took the phone from his hand, using her fingers to zoom in on Ducky's face. "This is him? He's very handsome, Chad." Her brow wrinkled as she glanced up. "You two have similar coloring, but your hair's darker now."

Chad nodded and looked down at Ducky's photo still on the screen. "He and I talk all the time. Mostly online and text, but it's moved to phone calls now too. We've never met face-to-face, but he's my best friend. I share almost everything with him, yet he didn't tell me he'd made these changes to his appearance. That's why I said it wasn't him during the podcast. It caught me off guard."

"Because you're attracted to him?" she asked, looking at the screen again, tapping it to keep the photo up.

"I was attracted to him before he did all this. He's a good guy, Mom. Smarter than anyone I know. We've been friends since we were on Xbox Live together in early junior high. I think he surpasses Dad with his knowledge of code. Ducky can hack into anything. We'd all be online together and watch him do it when we were younger." Chad took his phone from his mother, drawing her attention back to him. She needed to hear what he planned to say. "I've been dealing with my attraction to guys since way before Dad came out. Ducky was the first guy I was into. I've never stopped being into him. He's funny in this unintentional way, but he laughs at himself. He's real. The most real person I've ever known. I've never met anyone else like him."

"I never had any idea you had these feelings. When I asked the question, I didn't really expect this response," his mom said in that way only mothers used when they spoke of the regret of missing something so big. "You were young. You must have been afraid and unsure."

"Hell no, I wasn't afraid. Sorry," Chad said, ignoring the critical arching of her brow at the use of the swear word. "Do you think any child you raised could be afraid of anything?"

He pushed off the counter, tucking his cell phone back into his pocket. "I've been with guys, Mom. Lots of 'em. And that's all I'm going to say so don't ask me any questions." He couldn't contain the shiver running through him at the awkwardness of admitting even that much to his mother about his sex life.

"You've been with women, too. Right?" His mom stammered, clearly questioning everything she knew about Chad. "Don't answer that. It doesn't matter. How have I never known these things about you before? I tried to be an observant, present mother for your whole life. I love you." She looked pitiful, causing Chad to give a good laugh as his mother took her seat and lifted her glass of iced tea, taking several long gulps.

"Mom, all of us are very well-adjusted. You and Dad are great parents. Kids don't tell their parents everything. You know that. And it wasn't easy on any of us to have Dad's sexuality splashed out for the world to see. I get that social media doesn't hold weight, but when your father owns a social platform that's bought by a technology giant like Wilder and then those two men become a couple…the children involved are gonna get some backlash."

"Oh, I need something stronger than flavored tea." She went straight for the refrigerator. She had a glass of pinot noir poured in three point two seconds flat. "You should have warned me how serious this lunch date was going to get. I wasn't prepared. All I've ever wanted is for my children to have a good life. You're having a good life, right?"

She didn't wait for his answer. Instead, she took a long, several second gulp of the wine. Not quite draining the glass, but close.

"Of course, we have great lives." Although not one of his more recent problems was solved or even talked through for that matter, he felt much better watching his mother come to grips with his truth. "This is why we've kept that part of our lives to ourselves. Can we get back to my emotional breakdown before we deal with yours?"

This time, she tipped the glass back, draining the wine. As she filled another glass, fuller this time, she said, "Here's what I suggest. Talk to Ducky. Like your father always says, it's unfair to put your feelings into someone else's mouth, or however he says it." She waved a hand in the air. "You'd think I'd remember with as many times as I heard it. You know how he is with his sayings…"

"I can't talk to Ducky. He's not responding to me, Mom. Not one word. I feel like he's believing this crazy over-the-top reaction to what I said."

His normally quick thinking, articulate mother seemed to struggle for her words.

He waited while she took another drink.

"You're…" She sat the glass down and mimicked his stance from the other side of the counter, her hands placed on the granite as they again stared at one another. If he guessed right, she was still stuck on the problems he and his sisters had faced during their family's transition into this new way of life as a blended family life. Her face softened the longer she stared. "How different is this with Ducky compared to the others you've dated?"

"Very. All the feelings are there for me. I've managed to keep it hidden, telling myself I'd explore more when I was ready. I truly believe he's straight. I didn't want to ruin what we shared. Having him in my life a little is better than none at all."

"My son has strong feelings for someone, and I didn't know. How have I never heard this before?" She tossed her hands in the air again, then reached for the glass of wine.

"Focus, Mom." He snapped his fingers to get her attention back on him and pointed at himself. "Me first before this breakdown you're wanting to have."

"Okay." She looked away from Chad, staring off into the room as she spoke. "I suggest you take this in two steps. First, cross the imaginary boundary you have in place with Ducky. Go see him. He's in Grand Prairie, right?"

Chad nodded. Her perfectly arched brows lifted when her gaze came back to him.

"It's not far. Maybe twenty-five minutes away. Go to him today."

"All right," he said, unwilling to examine why he'd never let that be an option before.

"Explain to him that your words were a knee-jerk reaction. And apologize. See if what you feel carries over face-to-face, into everyday life. If it doesn't, you haven't ruined the friendship you have. If you still have these feelings, you need to tell him." She took another drink, watching him closely.

Chad blew out a breath, considering the idea. He didn't think he could stand for Ducky to push him away. "I don't know, Mom. I see the merit in the first part, but we'll have to see about the second."

She nodded and gave a little eye roll. "Let's go back to the other. What about Chloe and Cate? As far as I've known, they've only dated boys. Is that untrue?"

Yeah, he wasn't doing that. He left the counter separating them and gathered their lunch dishes to take to the sink. "I don't know about Cate, but Chloe's too hard to get along with. No one of any gender will ever want to date her."

He made quick work of dumping the dishes in the sink before pivoting around and kissing her cheek. "Thank you for the advice. I'll call Mark to pick up Cara. You don't need to drive."

He had to go home and change before he went down south to see Ducky. What did a person wear to impress their best friend? Something nice. He dragged his fingers through his hair as he went for the front door. He wished he had time for a quick spa run.

CHAPTER 8
FIND MY FRIENDS

Dread flooded Ducky, making his stomach roil. He absently rubbed a hand over his tight muscles, hoping to ease the nausea from the outside in. With the way the sweat trickled down his forehead, it had to be eighty degrees inside the small executive office. Skye's training classes were intense, but this was something different.

Maybe the mounting stacks of unfinished paperwork on his desk played a part in his anxiety. There was actual paper, like from a tree, on his desk. For an information technology geek, the growing mound of tree pulp sent a shiver down his spine.

The most likely culprit to this minute's severe frustration had to do with his brother's complete disregard of his wishes. Dallas had signed off on the advertising campaign that Ducky had wholeheartedly rejected.

While Ducky had smiled for the camera and rode the shit out of a spin bike to Skye's instruction, Dallas scoured over today's focus group reports revealing how they saw Ducky as relatable, genuine, and charming. *Yeah right!*

He'd bark out a laugh right now if his throat wasn't so dry with worry. Apparently his before and after full body shots made all those likable qualities even more endearing to the public at large.

Dallas hadn't even given Ducky a chance to digest this new information, and he didn't like that at all. His leg bounced as he stood directly behind Dallas's desk where Sara sat, finalizing the last details with their advertising agency.

"Stop pouting," Dallas murmured, standing close to Ducky as if he hadn't just stabbed the blade right in Ducky's back.

"It's really good, Ducky," Skye said from her perch on Dallas's desk, next to the monitor where she angled her body to view the computer screen. "If it was anyone but you in those pictures, you'd've made the same decision Dallas did. You're being hard to deal with for no reason."

"They think we can get ad space in Times Square." Sara jumped around in her seat with excitement, turning this way and that to see all three of their expressions. "There's a billboard opening. Do we want it? We want it, right?"

"Yes!" Skye said, jumping off the desk. Her boundless energy had her clapping her hands, joining in with Sara's enthusiasm.

"Absolutely," Dallas agreed, more sedate until Skye launched her body his way. Times Square must be some holy grail in the advertising world to get that sort of reaction from them.

"What's it gonna cost?" Ducky asked, looking between his two business partners as if they had lost their minds.

They always discussed the expense of everything before

making these kinds of decisions. Greer's bottom dollar approach played like an anthem in Ducky's mind. What was the return on this investment? Was it truly worth the cost or making an emotional decision because clearly with all the bouncing going on, emotions were at play. Yes, StreamTrainer made money, but expansion wasn't cheap. They couldn't just willy-nilly anything right now.

"Ducky, it's Times Square. StreamTrainer's gonna hit the big time. Yes, we can afford it," Skye teased, shooting out a hand to knock Ducky's shoulder. "How can we *not* afford it?"

"We can afford it. Right, Sara?" Dallas asked, finally showing some sign that his brother was still inside his body. About damn time he did.

Sara nodded and put a finger to her lips before she took the call off hold and finished with the advertising agency.

"It's done. We need to celebrate," Sara said, placing her cell phone on the desk. She pushed back in the office chair, sliding right between where Ducky and Dallas stood. Her hands went up for high fives all the way around. Of course, he didn't participate. Ducky rolled his eyes, keeping his arms tightly crossed over his chest as he pivoted away from the group.

The deep inner embarrassment of having his face and body up in lights for the world to see was his cross to bear. The field day his buddies were going to have at his expense made the mortification run deeper.

Speaking of his friends, he hadn't checked in with anyone in days. If he was smart, he'd start preparing them to get ahead of the teasing. His gaze scanned his desk for his cell phone. He had no idea where it was. How had this become his life?

Work for yourself, they said.

It was more fulfilling, they argued.

What a joke.

A yawn slipped free. He was too tired to really absorb the impact of what they had just done. His arms fell to his sides as he pulled his chair out and dropped into the seat in utter defeat. In hindsight, he should've told The Game Awards he wasn't interested in presenting this year. Never started down this path to begin with. He liked his old self well enough.

"Ducky, let's go eat," Dallas said as if Ducky's only job was to follow his instruction. Couldn't Dallas see how tired he was of people running all over him? He cast a glance over his shoulder as his brother shrugged on his suit coat. Skye stood beside him, zipping her logoed StreamTrainer jacket.

"You pick the place," Skye added as an incentive, flipping her ponytail out the back.

"Y'all go without me. I have all this to do." Ducky swept a hand over the pile on his desk, indicating the mounds of work awaiting him.

"It'll be here tomorrow," Skye said, nodding her head toward the open office door.

He answered by reaching down to boot up his computer, hoping they got the message. Seconds later, Dallas's hand landed on his shoulder, giving a gentle squeeze. His other hand brought a long envelope forward, putting it in Ducky's line of vision where he couldn't see anything else. "You don't have to go with us tonight. I know you're mad at me, but Skye and I agreed you needed this gift. We planned to give it to you at dinner before I messed it up by going around you like I did."

Skye's pretty penmanship scrolled the words *Thank you, Ducky* on the pale purple envelope.

He turned in his chair, taking the card while looking between the both of them. The irritation faded a tinge. He slid a finger under the flap, loosening the tight seal. A greeting card with a caricature of a girl in a hula skirt, a cow chewing at the grass of her skirt, slid out.

The card read Moo Chew Grass-ias.

"What's this?"

Dallas tucked both his hands in his slacks pockets, rocking back on his heels. Clearly, proud of his gift. "You've worked nonstop since we started this in our tiny apartment, and you've never taken more than a single day off."

A folded piece of paper fell to his lap from the card. It held an itinerary and two first-class plane tickets. "A trip to Hawaii?"

"Not just a trip. It's a *perfect vacation* trip to Hawaii," Skye interjected. "It's gorgeous there. They have these villas right off the water. It can be quiet when you need the peace and has a fun night life. We included a two-week reservation in a private villa with two bedrooms. We want you to go. Take a break and get away. Rejuvenate."

"We know all this attention you're getting is taking its toll. Then I didn't help matters," Dallas said, throwing a hand back to his desk, indicating the exact place Ducky had had the rug pulled out from underneath him. "And you've earned it. Get away and let this happen. When you get back, this will have calmed down."

"Hawaii must've cost a fortune," Ducky said, looking up at Dallas. His brain misfired as he processed even more new information thrown at him today, not entirely sure how he felt about this new turn of events.

"Don't look like that. We paid for it out of our pockets. This is from Greer, Skye, and me. Not the business," Dallas said.

"I don't know if it's the right time," Ducky hedged, deciding he'd think about the trip tomorrow after a good night's sleep. Besides, which friend did he take? If he asked someone on his gaming team, then another player would get their feelings hurt. Yeah, maybe this was a bad idea. "I've got all this work to do plus Sara's schedule has me starting at five in the morning. We're doing *Good Morning America*," Ducky explained, tossing the card and the itinerary on his desk.

"Delegate. You deserve the time off to relax, Ducky," Skye encouraged, nodding to drive her point home. She slapped Dallas on the arm. "Let him think about it. Come on. I'm starving." That was Skye's code to Dallas to leave him alone and let him work through everything on his own.

The weight of Dallas's hand came back to rest on his shoulder, he squeezed again in a brotherly way. "I know you're outside your comfort zone. I only signed off because I also know you can handle it. I promise that campaign's the best we've ever had. Go away, relax, then come back ready to hit the ground running."

Dallas didn't wait for an answer, he hooked an arm through Skye's and they left with Sara again joining them just beyond their office door with her purse in hand. They must have planned dinner as a group event. He watched them until he couldn't see them anymore then stared longer, recognizing the feeling of burnout and constant frustration that was so unlike him.

The quest for his misplaced cell phone came back to the forefront. Where did he leave the dang thing? The locker room? Ducky got to his feet and started in that direction.

Maybe a vacation wasn't such a bad idea.

The creepy feeling of being a stalker only added to the worry that drove Chad to StreamTrainer's corporate offices. He took the turn into the parking lot, glancing inside each of the three vehicles headed out. The only person he recognized was Dallas Reigns in a Tesla. He lifted a hand, hoping to appear as if he were expected to be there instead of using a location app to track Ducky's whereabouts.

Time had sped up on him this afternoon. After learning his stepfather was too tied up at work to pick up Cara, Chad went back to drive his tipsy mother to pick up his sister from school—the exact thing he'd tried to avoid. Then he'd gone home, showered, cleaned himself up before fussing over his clothing. He wanted to look his very best, choosing his most expensive apparel items in hopes that cost tipped the scale on how he looked. Chad had most certainly lost his mind. He'd clocked in at over two hours before he left his condo in Dallas and made his way thirty minutes to Ducky's office.

StreamTrainer had workout sessions going twenty-four/seven. Chad pulled past the training entrance to the front offices. If the barren parking lot was an indicator, maybe he'd catch Ducky alone. With a wide swing of the vehicle, Chad parked in the first spot, facing the foyer of the building. The small space looked packed with empty cubicles. An armed security guard stood just inside the front doors.

Chad glanced down at his outfit. Maybe he'd overdressed. He should come back tomorrow now that he had a feel for the casual nature of the office. Training clothes would have been a better option than the tieless suit he'd chosen. What had he been thinking?

"Stop second-guessing yourself and get out of the car." The words echoed around the silence of his vehicle, startling even him.

He flipped down the visor to look into the small mirror. As he matured, his hair had lost a lot of the natural red highlights, leaving behind this darker shade, almost black like his mother and sisters. His close-cropped facial hair made his slate-blue eyes look lighter than they were.

Why the hell was he so nervous about seeing Ducky? He'd stared Ducky in the eyes while online for years, doing it face-to-face shouldn't be any different. Yet somehow it was.

He reached for the door handle and pushed it open before turning off the engine. He glanced at himself in the mirror one last time. "You're taking this in steps. First, apologize, and hopefully get the friendship back on track. That's your goal tonight."

With courage he didn't really possess, he stepped out of the car and straightened his clothes before he squared his shoulders and slammed the door with a little more force than he'd intended. Normally, he treated his new Range Rover as if it were a baby. This evening, it was the last thing on his mind.

Taking long, sure strides, Chad rushed to the front doors, pulling one open to be greeted with a single nod by the no nonsense security guard. He said nothing as he entered the building, obviously waiting for Chad to speak first.

"I'm looking for Ducky, Duncan Reigns. Is he around?" Chad instinctively reached for his wallet, pulling out his driver's license, handing it to the guard.

After what felt like a long perusal of the guard looking at him then down to his identification, he handed it back and cocked his head toward the desk. "He went toward the locker rooms. I'll call for him," the guard said, taking a step toward the empty desk in the foyer.

"No, that's okay. I'll go find him." He waved the guard off, tucking the driver's license back inside the wallet then placing that inside his inside breast pocket. His gaze followed the sign on the wall pointing him to the direction of the locker room.

He'd barely made it around the corner when Ducky stepped into the hall from the other direction, head bent, cell phone in his hand, his thumbs working over the screen.

Chad stopped dead in his tracks as he stared at the man who had fascinated him for half of his life. Ducky had on his workout gear, fitted shorts, and a snug tank top that left little to the imagination of what was underneath. Chad couldn't speak nor could he take his eyes off the man in front of him.

All he managed was to stand there like the creeper he'd become and openly stare at his gorgeous friend. Ducky was tall, really tall. His skin tanner than Chad remembered ever seeing before and the guy was as beautifully handsome on the outside as he was on the inside. Ducky had an air of gentle masculinity that called to Chad on so many levels. His heart fluttered against his rib cage. His breathing became labored as he again absorbed the visceral reaction to Ducky.

The overwhelming attraction hit him like a ton of bricks, bowling him over, at least with the way the neurons misfired inside his brain.

The earth tilted. It felt like the rug had been pulled from under his feet. Chad's stance became unsteady as Ducky took steps toward him. Any lingering uncertainty about his attraction settled as Ducky walked toward him. He needed Ducky Reigns like he needed air. His heart yearned, demanding he make this happen between them.

His breath held. The sound of his heart pounded loudly in his ears as he waited for his friend to notice him. He watched as Ducky did a distracted glance up then down again, doing something on his phone before stopping in his tracks and looking back up at him. When those captivating eyes locked on to him, Chad's world zoomed back into focus on this moment.

He found his life's purpose and meaning in the depths of Ducky's sparkling green stare.

Please. Please be into guys, or maybe just into me.

He liked the last part of his thought the most.

The bond of their friendship, and the connection he shared with Ducky, swirled around them, charging the air with sudden intensity. He wondered if Ducky felt it too. Ducky's grin was immediate. He started to walk again, stopping about a foot from Chad. If his friend noticed the energy between them, he didn't let on.

"I just texted you." As if on a cosmic cue, Chad's cell phone vibrated against his chest.

He did grin, but as he opened his mouth to speak, nothing came out. His throat, tongue, and lips suddenly became dry and heavy, forcing him to close his mouth and clear his throat. The buzzing in his head made it hard to think.

"I…" He had to look away from Ducky to make his brain function properly. The attraction to his friend combined with his nerves made it hard to think let alone speak. Holy hell, his palms were sweaty. He fisted them as he tucked both hands into his slacks pockets. "I hadn't heard from you. I texted a lot since the podcast. You're one of my best friends, I don't want you to be mad at me. I didn't mean what I said…"

Ducky lifted his cell, waving it back and forth. The giant grin and ease of Ducky's facial features were still in place. "I saw all of your apologies." Ducky's tone said Chad had been silly for thinking what he had. He started walking again, passing Chad.

Chad's gaze ran the length of Ducky's body, taking it all in. Strong shoulders, a small firm waist, muscular carved legs, and a mouthwatering ass. His knees almost buckled as he took a step. His cock hardened so quickly it hurt. He gathered his lapels, buttoning his jacket in place to hide the damning evidence of his arousal.

"Why would I be mad? Come to my office. Everyone's gone. We'll be alone there which is hard to find around here these days."

Chad followed Ducky, something he hoped to do a lot of in the future.

"It's good. He's a friend," Ducky said, probably to the security guard. He didn't know for sure because he couldn't take his eyes off Ducky's ass.

Ducky had a strut. *Interesting.* Chad was mesmerized, watching Ducky's tempting ass sway with each step he took. He had to look away again to concentrate on Ducky's words.

"Dallas, Skye, and I share this office. We're getting new space." Ducky looked over his shoulder at Chad as he entered the office, grinning as he spread his arms out to encompass the packed space as if to show he wasn't exaggerating. He let Chad walk in and shut the door behind them.

The funk he had been living under for days now disappeared. Left behind was an energy buzzing between him and Ducky. An unseen connection drew him to Ducky.

It was physical and binding and totally confusing. "You've changed."

"I did. I put on almost twenty pounds of muscle since I started. Lost the fat and made Greer dress me," Ducky said, chuckling. If he read all the signs correctly, his friend was as unaffected by Chad's presence as Chad was affected. He stifled a groan of frustration worried that the earth moving emotions coursing through him were only happening for him. Life was just that cruel. "I told you I liked his clothes, but I didn't like them quite as much once they were on me."

"You wore Greer's clothes," Chad asked, barely following the conversation trail as his mind stayed stuck in processing his own emotions. Ducky passed by him, going for one of the three desks in the small room. Of course, Chad could tell which desk was Ducky's. The multiple monitors and enormous computer gave the secret away.

Ducky's scent mixed with a cologne he couldn't quite name and the hints of musk from sweat. Chad bit his lower lip, digging the smell as he turned to follow Ducky, taking the seat Ducky pushed out for him.

"No. He did my clothing makeover. I wore the suit Greer picked out to The Game Awards." Ducky plopped down in his seat then sent his chair rolling to a small refrigerator under his desk. "Want a cold water?"

"I'm good, but can you leave?" Chad asked on nothing but instinct. "Want to have dinner? I feel like there's a lot to catch up on."

Ducky took a water, twisting the top as he nodded toward his desk and smiled. There were piles of paperwork there. Ducky stood as he gulped the water. "Yeah, I'm starving, but I'll do you one better than dinner. You busy for the next couple of weeks?"

Chad had no idea what leap Ducky just took inside his head, but he went with it. "I don't know…" Literally, his to-do list ran pages long. Number one being to deal with his golfing career. "Why are you asking?"

"Let me go change before we bounce," Ducky said, handing over an envelope from his desk as he passed by. "Take a look. I'll be out in a sec."

The contents spilled into his hands. The location and itinerary had him lifting his brows. "Hawaii, are you kidding?"

"They just gave it to me as a gift. If you can't go, it's fine. I didn't commit to going yet," Ducky called out.

He had two prepaid, first-class airline tickets in his hand and a reservation for a private villa on the beach for fourteen days.

Their exchange was given so casually. Chad had to rewind the conversation in his mind to make sense of what he was holding. Had Ducky invited him to an all-expenses paid vacation in Hawaii? Like them together in Hawaii by themselves?

.

CHAPTER 9
SKILLS

Ducky sidled up to a vintage bar, scuffed from years of loyal customers doing the very same thing. Bruno's Bar and Grill. A hometown favorite and the last place he had worked before quitting to focus solely on StreamTrainer. Since Ducky had fallen headfirst into a world that changed by the second, this spot at the end of the bar felt like home.

Having Chad take the seat next to him was a different story. Sometimes when Ducky met his strictly online friends face-to-face, the connection they shared didn't hold true in their real life. The relationship changed afterward. He'd feared those consequences if he'd ever met Chad in person. What did a poor kid from Grand Prairie, Texas, have in common with the obscene wealth of someone from Highland Park? But after the last thirty minutes, maybe those fears didn't hold weight. Chad was as comfortable to be around in person as he was behind the screen or over the phone.

"This is the famous Bruno's," Chad said, rolling up his

dress shirt's long sleeves.

Ducky watched, fascinated with the sophistication that poured from Chad Reeves. Even with the way he took each sleeve and carefully folded the material over and over, Chad did it with style. He cared for the pressed fabric in much the same way as Greer did.

He better understood owning the clothes, not letting the clothes own him. Chad respected the material without shoving the rich fabric in everyone's face. It went deeper though. Chad was comfortable in his own skin. Something Ducky didn't fully grasp.

Ducky focused on Chad's hands as they worked. They were strong, adept, and moved fluidly without Chad even paying attention to what he was doing. Chad lifted a hand, waving it in front of Ducky's face. "You there?"

See? Life wasn't fluid for Ducky in that way. He shrugged it off by admitting the truth. It seemed the best answer. "Yeah. I'm fried."

"We don't have to do this," Chad immediately responded, concern wrinkling his brow. He had the perfect coloring. His skin tone complimented his dark eyebrows. Ducky's gaze followed his friend's perfectly arched brows as they dipped lower, and those full lips melted into a frown.

Chad had always been hands down the best-looking guy in their online group. As children, they'd talk about their futures. Their whole world centered on the chicks they planned to meet. They designated Chad as the one to draw those unsuspecting girls in. Kai, the ultimate wingman, would then help charm those little ladies to keep them around. Ducky's job was to stay quiet and let them work. They'd generously dubbed Ducky as aloof and mysterious. Right.

"No, I'm glad you're here," he said, reaching for the bowl of pretzels nearby. "I was remembering how we used to plan on getting girlfriends. Remember our strategy?"

Chad immediately grinned, nodding. His lips spread, revealing a brilliant toothy smile. Teeth white and straight. He bet Chad had never had a cavity in his life. "You were going to be the best wingman ever."

Ducky barked out a laugh and lifted a hand to catch the bartender's attention. "I think that was Kai. The rest of us were to sit quietly and reap the spoils of what you two brought in."

"It didn't turn out like we thought, did it?" Chad asked, his full attention on Ducky. That was another thing Chad did so well. He always gave his undivided attention.

Before Ducky could answer, Betty the bartender came over, putting a Diet Coke in front of Ducky. "Saw you on that award show. We had a viewing party here in the bar. You were solid." Betty reached a fist over the bar, giving Ducky a quick knuckle touch. A whistle came from the other end of the bar where a single pool table and dart board resided. The busboy, another longtime friend, gave a loud whoop that started a round of applause from the smattering of regular customers. He recognized most of them.

"Okay, okay, calm down," Ducky said, swiveling toward the room. The silliness had him grinning. "It wasn't that big a deal. I said like fifteen words."

"Wasn't sure you had those fifteen words in you," Betty teased and looked at Chad, eyeing him close. "Ducky was nervous and not known to be articulate…" Her gaze narrowed when she leaned forward to study Chad's face closer. "You're the guy who insisted that it wasn't Ducky on stage."

Chad's hands lifted in surrender. "I knew it was him. I just hadn't seen the change. He looks like a different man. I was defending the OG Ducky. That's all."

Betty, always ready to give Ducky shit, changed her critical tone and backed off Chad. "Right? Not only the looks. He acts completely different than I've ever known. Everybody here talks about it. When he used to work here, he rarely spoke a word to anyone. He always worked with his music blaring in one ear. You'd look over and see him headbanging to some unknown sound. Now he has himself on stage giving out awards?"

This was his comfortable place, his home away from home. Ducky went along with what Betty said, nodding at the truth she spoke. "This is the only job I had that didn't care that I left my earbud in." He tossed a thumb toward Chad. "He knows my long, sordid history with work. I have a collection of hairnets and name tags. Wasn't really my thing."

Betty barked out a laugh at his honesty. "Do we still need to pretend that you aren't eating here?" Betty gave her best shit-giving grin to Chad as if she'd finally revealed something top-secret. "He got himself a fancy chef to cook healthy meals but sneaks in here under the cloak of night to eat a burger and fries."

"You have a personal chef?" Chad asked in disbelief.

Ducky frowned when he said, "My brother and his boyfriend really got behind this change in me. My life's become protein shakes, workouts, and eating lots of lean meats and greens. It takes so much mental energy to be healthy. How does anyone do it?"

"Didn't you ask for their help?" Chad asked. The tone indicated Ducky must have gotten what he deserved.

"Hey now, watch it. All I asked Greer to do was help me dress for the award show. I had no idea I was going to have to do all this. The guy's unstoppable," Ducky explained, sitting back on his seat, crossing his arms over his chest. He barely kept the disgruntled *humph* from slipping out.

"Don't get pissy. It can't be that big a burden. You're fire now. Can Greer get a hold of me? I'm sure there's a beauty underneath all these wrinkles," Betty teased. A loud cackle followed. "I swear, all the good ones are either taken or gay. What do you want to drink?"

Chad chuckled at the quick turn in the conversation and glanced back toward Ducky. "What're you drinking?"

"This is a Diet Coke but have what you want." Ducky picked up his newest drink of choice, taking a hearty gulp.

"I'll have the same thing but make it a real Coke. I can't drink tonight; I have precious cargo to get home."

Oh jeez. Betty grinned, falling for the sweet sentiment implied in Chad's silly comment about driving him home when they finished. She gave Ducky a knowing wink. The charm dripping from Chad made Betty's face soften, which might be a first in all the time he'd known her. "He's a keeper, Duck-man. So he's probably gay too. Right?"

Everyone within hearing distance burst out with laughter.

"Same as always, right?" she asked, Ducky nodded. "You ready to order?"

Chad cut his playful gaze toward Ducky. "I'm guessing your regular is the forbidden hamburger, cooked medium, fully loaded with mustard, no ketchup."

"You know him well," Becky answered for Ducky.

"I'll have the same thing but put cheese on mine." Chad gave a confirming nod as if the secret to Ducky's diet rested solely between the three of them. He was so damned smooth all the time. Betty ate right out of Chad's palm. No one stood a chance against Chad. She nodded, and scooped ice into a glass then filled the soda, passing it over with a wink.

Emma, a woman Ducky went to high school with, came to the edge of the bar and pulled out a chair to sit on the other side of Chad. Her elbow went to the middle of the bar. She put her head in her hand, all her attention focused on Chad. "You know, I was really upset with you for being so rude about Ducky. Then here you come, strolling in with Ducky like y'all are best friends. I think we're gonna need to know what happened if you want a shot at forgiveness." She tried her best to look playfully menacing. She cast a quick glance over her shoulder at the rest of the patrons in the bar as if they were in on her distaste. "You should also know, I've said some pretty bad things about you on Secret."

Chad nodded solemnly, as if taking her threat seriously. "I think I became the most hated man in the world for a minute there."

"Oh yeah," another customer piped in from a table behind them. Ducky glanced over his shoulder, lifting his chin at another familiar face. "He needs to explain himself before we all sit in here like nothing happened."

Ducky opened his mouth to respond, not liking how they put Chad on blast, but Chad laughed and lifted a hand to Ducky, indicating he'd take care of this. He turned in his seat toward the entire bar as if braving a firing squad. "Okay. Okay. Let me plead my case. This is what really happened…"

In a series of events that had become genuinely real and

authentic, Chad chalked this exact moment up as being his new number one favorite memory of the night. Ducky expertly aligned his body with the dartboard and sent the dart flying.

As with all the others he threw before, it landed exactly where Ducky chose it to, solidly beating Chad at their game.

The bar-goers watched and cheered for Ducky, not nearly as surprised at Ducky's skill as Chad. "Wait. Unfair. I've been hustled," he complained loudly, only making the cheers grow louder.

Ducky's side grin, the one he gave while trying to hide his humor, shot over his shoulder toward him and the rest of his adoring audience before he turned away from the floor mark and came back to their table. Ducky shrugged as he took his stool, sliding on top. "I can teach you how to play if you want."

The comeback hit as intended. Chad barked out a laugh as he lifted his glass of ice water, taking a drink to help swallow his defeat. "Yeah, yeah. You're hiding so many secrets. All these years and I never heard one single word about you being a dartist. You know, I'm considered a decent player in some circles."

Ducky's loud laugh revealed how hilarious he found that statement, which had a twofold effect on Chad. One of the things he'd always liked about Ducky was that bold laugh. It spoke of many things. This time though was Chad's second issue. The hilarity of the laugh made it clear that Ducky didn't believe Chad had any skill at darts.

"Okay, okay," Chad lifted his hands in surrender, giving a playful eye roll. "I might need you to give me a lesson or two. How'd you get so good?"

"While your dad was gently teaching you the love of

sports, my dad taught all three of us how to hustle. We shoot pool, play cards, and throw darts. He'd teach us just enough to still beat us soundly every time we got together. We all got super competitive. Don't ever let Dallas corner you in a game of pool. I'm better at darts. My oldest brother Donny is a card shark," Ducky explained, lifting his almost empty glass, letting the ice cubes fall into his mouth. He chomped on those, discarding the glass back on the table. "I've got to go to the bathroom then I should head home. I'm exhausted."

His gaze followed Ducky's retreat until he disappeared down the hall leading to the bathroom. He released a pent-up sigh and turned back in his seat. More than anything, he wished he could toss the contents of his glass of ice water into his heated face. The strain of all his unrequited desire was taking its toll. He needed to move, walk off this hard-on, if that were even possible.

Chad left their table, walking a measured twenty steps back to the bar top to settle their bill. Interestingly, those steps didn't help relieve anything.

The judgment he'd been hit with when they first arrived had dissolved into a really nice time. These people were as genuine as Ducky. They had easily given Chad a second chance for no other reason than they were good people. He'd enjoyed tonight. Glad he listened to his mother's advice.

He fished his wallet from his back pocket and thumbed through the cash. The bartender laid the tab out for him to see. "Ducky has an account here."

"I'll pay," he answered distractedly, looking down at the small total circled at the bottom, which was much less than he'd expected. Two burgers, fries, drinks, and darts had cost him less than thirty dollars. This place just got better and better.

"You're awfully nice-looking," Betty said, drawing Chad's attention. She was absently wiping across the bar top with a terry cloth towel, still eyeing him as he laid forty dollars on the ticket.

"Are you trying to increase your tip?" he teased.

He laid a few more dollar bills down, fully aware he was leaving a forty percent tip. Not because of her words or that he was a great tipper, but he truly appreciated her friendliness.

Stepping closer, she grinned. "Yeah, worked too." She swiped the money away before he could change his mind. "I see the way you're looking at him."

"Oh yeah? How's that?" he asked, tucking his wallet back inside his pants pocket.

"Like you want to pay his way." Since her sarcastic personality had rarely given him a break all evening, her answer surprised him. Warmth creeped up his neck as he lost eye contact, ducking his head, wishing he hadn't been so transparent.

"Is it obvious?"

"Oh yeah," one of the waitresses said as she came to stand next to him at the bar. "You look at Ducky like he's a piece of steak. I get it. He sure changed his appearance since he and I went out."

That confession caught Chad's full attention. He glanced over at her, getting a closer look. She was tall, taller than Ducky, and lanky. Her gauged earlobes and many piercings accentuated her goth vibe. Her eyes were outlined in deep black liner. He bet she and Ducky shared the same taste in metal music.

"When did you date?" Chad asked.

Before she had a chance to answer, he heard Ducky say from his other side, "I have an account here. It's covered. You don't have to pay."

"He already paid and tips better than you," Betty said with a cackle. "I'll take his money over yours every time."

Ducky's hands flew into the air in an I-give-up gesture. He turned for the front door. "Now you're making me look bad, Reeves. Can't believe it's me at the awards, over-tipping my people to show you have deeper pockets..." Ducky couldn't hold the line of his words for the laughter that erupted behind him. "I gotta hit the sack. Let's go."

Here he was, destined to always follow Ducky wherever he led.

CHAPTER 10
YEAH

"I'm glad to see he's smiling again," Dallas said loudly as he entered their shared office space.

He pretended not to hear, speedily typing notes into the StreamTrainer proprietary software. A program he created from scratch and fine-tuned every day for the past two years. His gaze moved to his second monitor, scanning the screen, watching the activity from their social users. Their moderators were good at their jobs, promoting their community standards throughout the entire platform. His fingers flew over the keyboard, knowing all the command prompts by heart to pull his calendar up and adding a reminder to let them know what a good job they were doing.

"He's back to what he really wants to do," Skye added. The quirk of the corner of Ducky's lip showed he'd heard her. "You can change a man, lead him to the promised land, but can't make him bite."

"I feel like you mixed several unrelated metaphors to form that sentence," Ducky said, never breaking from work.

"I signed Texas Health Resources this morning. They'll go into effect in ninety days. They have twenty-four thousand employees, estimating about seven thousand units will be sold through their benefits package," Dallas said, placing his key fob and cell phone on his desk. A file folder followed, then a squeak sounded when Dallas took his chair.

"Type up the specifics as soon as you can so we can get them in the system. I'll review the charges and implementation when I get back," Ducky said distractedly over his shoulder.

When he spoke, the beep in his ear drew his gaze down to the open chat box in the corner of the screen. He gave an almost silent laugh when Chad posted a picture of his heavy ski coat, suggesting it as an appropriate wardrobe choice for their sun and sand vacation, on which they were leaving tomorrow.

That message came after Ducky explained he hadn't even considered clothing options for the trip. Outside of his workout gear, he didn't have anything suitable to wear except the shorts and T-shirts he'd owned forever. He was going to have to do a Target run when he left tonight to gather what he needed to pack for the flight tomorrow.

With a click of the mouse, he pulled the chat box to the center of the screen and typed, *"I haven't been to Hawaii, but I feel like that's a solid choice."*

The three drumming dots appeared again, and Ducky lifted his fingers from his keyboard, his gaze focused only on the impending message. He didn't have to wait long. *"Great. I have snow pants that match the jacket."* That message came with another immediately after. *"I feel like I should be paying my way."*

Yeah, Chad couldn't let that go. From the moment they had agreed on taking the trip, Chad had started insisting he pay his half. No amount of explaining seemed to penetrate Chad's single-minded focus. He typed again. *"This is on Dallas. Besides, he needs to pay for what he did to me."*

Ducky held back his grumble about the ad campaign, his annoyance still very real.

As if he'd read Ducky's unrelenting aggravation with his brother in those words, Chad replied, *"Yeah, yeah. Did you find out when the ad starts running? I need to see what's got you so bent,"* Chad replied.

He just shook his head as if Chad could see him. *"No, you don't. I keep telling you that too. No one needs to see the ad campaign. I'm pissed about it. I think I was fine looking in the before pictures."*

"I do too." Chad one hundred percent had his back about this advertising campaign since the first moment he'd mentioned it. Having Chad voice his support helped strengthen Ducky's resolve that he'd been the wronged party on their executive team.

He'd always had Dallas's back. Always. Maybe their bond wasn't as solid as he thought.

Ducky drew in a breath, recalibrating his thoughts. Dallas was right. Ducky needed to lose the salty attitude. He should consider StreamTrainer above all else.

"He's not listening again. Is the music cranked up?" Dallas asked, his raised voice drawing Ducky back into the room.

"I don't think so." Skye rose in her chair to get a closer look at Ducky. He caught her move in his peripheral vision. "He's been on chat a lot today."

"Y'all mind your business," Ducky said.

They weren't wrong though. He still had a ton of work to do before leaving in the morning. With that reminder, he quickly typed, *"I gotta bounce. I'll meet you at the airport in the morning."*

The drumming dots wiggled across the screen, and Ducky was shit to do anything more than wait. *"You sure you don't want a ride?"*

Another cool thing about Chad was that he never questioned Ducky's reason for choosing not to drive himself. So many times, the people in his life condensed his complete existence to the fact he couldn't drive, but Chad accepted his decision and moved on. He always had. *"Nah, I have a car picking me up first thing in the morning. Thanks tho."*

"If it changes, let me know. Otherwise, I'll probably end up texting you later. You seem to be the only person I want to talk to right now."

His heart smiled at the words on the screen. His lips most likely followed suit. *"Same,"* Ducky typed. Maybe this vacation was exactly what he needed. To get away meant a chance to rejuvenate. Something he desperately craved.

The Uber driver did little more than pop the trunk from his driver's side seat. "Safe travels."

Of course, Chad would get his own bag. He only had a duffle and computer bag, but the guy didn't even pretend to exit the car to help. Much like when the driver had first arrived to pick him up from his condo.

"Thanks," Chad muttered, reaching for the door handle. His cell phone rang before his feet were firmly planted on the pavement. He tapped his earpiece, shutting the car's door and answered blindly, assuming it was Ducky. Chad was only about five minutes behind schedule, but Ducky did everything dependably on time.

"I'm at the airport. Coming inside now," Chad said, taking the straps to both bags and throwing them over his shoulder before closing the trunk. He glanced toward the airport, looking for the entrance and had one foot up the curb when Tristan's voice threw him off balance.

"Are you expecting to pick me up from the airport?" Tristan's voice held a hint of confusion as Chad's foot slid off the curb, sending him pitching forward. He barely stayed on his feet.

"No. No, no. I thought you were someone else. I'm headed to Hawaii. I thought I told y'all," Chad said, all forward movement coming to a complete stop. He stared inside the arrival entrance windows while rooted to his spot. Chad cringed. Maybe he hadn't told his fathers about this trip. Things had turned awkward with Tristan. He had no idea if Tristan kept his secret or not. Which meant he hadn't talked to his dad in over a week. His mind started ticking off backward, trying to remember their last conversation.

"Hawaii?" Tristan asked. "That's a nice trip."

"Yeah." His only reply.

"All right, son, I won't keep you. I know you haven't agreed to take the Wilder Sports position, but I'm moving forward as if you have. The benefit of working with family," Tristan teased, needing no encouragement to laugh at his own joke. "Since signing Kai, we've had almost twelve hundred applications from athletes to be considered for sponsorship. We've vetted about twenty or so athletes as possibilities. I'm going to loop you in on these. I also assigned you as interim head of the department. I need this off my plate. I have too much going on myself. If you decide against the position, we'll replace you as soon as possible. The responsibility and salary for interim head is the same as what I offered you."

"I…" Chad sucked his lower lip between his teeth, looking down at the small divots and cracks in the concrete. He hadn't even considered the position since working things out with Ducky. His whole focus was enmeshed in the two goals he'd made for himself with his mother's help.

"Hey," Ducky said, startling him. His gaze collided with the green eyes that filled his dreams and spoke of deep friendship, trust, and patience. Ducky's easy grin slipped into place, and Chad had to fight the urge to lean in to kiss his friend. "Oh, sorry, I didn't see you were on the phone. Traffic was a bitch."

"Is that Ducky?" Tristan asked.

"Yeah." The single word sounded guarded, probably more so to Tristan than Chad wanted it to.

"Are you two going to Hawaii?"

"Yeah." Again, the single syllable spoke volumes more if Tristan dared to read between the lines.

"Huh."

"Yeah." He sounded like a broken record. The awkwardness between them elevated several notches. *Think.* Say something more to Tristan's complete silence. "He was gifted a trip by his brother. He invited me to go."

The crickets on the other end had Chad closing his eyes and waiting.

"Tell Ducky I said hello. You two have fun. If you can take a look at these candidates, it would help me out."

"I can do that," he replied, relieved nothing more was said. "I brought my laptop. I can head up WS, and I'll let you know my decision pretty quick. I've been distracted."

"Take your time. No pressure. I'm sending you a series of emails. One from Human Resources to get you set up."

Tristan was back to all business. "I'm assuming your father doesn't know about your vacation or I would have heard. Don't rat me out."

"Got it," Chad replied, feeling back on steadier ground. A porter came forward and spoke directly to Ducky who motioned for Chad to follow. "I've got to go. I'll take care of it all once we're settled in Hawaii."

"Sure thing," Tristan said, his teasing tone was back. "Let me know how it goes. I'm hanging up now before you tell me something I'll never believe about you and Ducky. Bye."

The call ended.

"Chad, over here," Ducky called out, waving a hand to get his attention. "Did you want to keep your laptop bag with you?"

This sense of new beginnings hanging over him, empowered him to move forward, immediately finding his way back to his happy place. No matter how the next few weeks played out, when he stepped back on Texas soil, he'd be a different man. The change was filled with anticipation, growth, and resolve. Dare he hope that he and Ducky might find their way together. The last one landed squarely in the farfetched category, but a guy could dream.

Whatever happened, he looked forward to the new direction of his life.

CHAPTER 11
CARBS

"They didn't hold back, did they?" Ducky said, letting go of his suitcase. His laptop bag slid off his shoulder, the strap falling down his arm until it too lay on the tiled floor. He was barely inside the doorway as he soaked in his surroundings. Tranquility wrapped in opulence. The villa Dallas had leased might be the coolest home he'd ever seen.

The modern open-plan layout allowed anyone who entered to immerse themselves in the bright turquoise waters, enticing beach, and lush green mountains just beyond the living room windows. The light-colored tile and matching interior furnishings enhanced the tropical view. He'd love to own a place like this someday.

"Seriously," Chad said, following Ducky deeper inside the villa. When Ducky stopped in the middle of the living room, Chad bypassed him, going straight for the patio. The back wall of windows retracted as Chad pushed buttons on the wall to open the living room to the lanai, making it one big room. "There's a swimming pool that runs the length of the back deck. I've never seen anything like this before."

Ducky followed, lost to the view of the ocean just feet away. Dallas hadn't lied when he'd said they'd booked a private getaway. Landscaping decorated the length of either side of the villa blocking the view inside the home from anyone else to see. He took a deep breath, letting the clean ocean air fill his lungs. The sound of waves meeting the pristine shore along with the bright cloudless sky filled his soul, easing away the stresses of his life.

If they ever considered relocating StreamTrainer's corporate headquarters, they needed to move right there, inside that rental property. Movement on the beach caught his eye. He hadn't even heard Chad run down the ramp to the beach. He stood there watching as Chad kicked off his shoes and flung his T-shirt wildly into the air. Chad sprinted toward the ocean. His cargo shorts hit the wet sand about a yard from where the surf edged toward shore.

The moment hit Ducky like a sledgehammer to the heart. Worse than even on the plane ride, sitting next to the man and his magnificent cologne. He'd been certain if wealth had a fragrance, it smelled like Chad Reeves.

Time slowed. Chad's extraordinary body was all he saw. A frame that perfect could only be made so hard and muscular by years of working out and competing athletically in the world. His flawless ass swung back and forth with each stride he took. The guy had no inhibitions whatsoever. *Jeez.*

"Come in," Chad yelled over his shoulder. Ducky got a brief glance of Chad's smiling face before he dove headfirst into the water. The moment of peace was lost as desire raced throughout every vein in Ducky's body. Ducky crossed his arms over his chest, and let his head fall back between his shoulders. He stared unseeing at the blue sky. What had he been thinking when inviting Chad to come along?

Chad of all people. A deep disgruntled sigh escaped.

He hadn't thought this out properly. He was going to be in a state of needy arousal the entire trip. This wasn't going to be a relaxing vacation. Instead, it would be a torturous lesson in self-control. He rolled his eyes and looked at the ocean in search of his friend. Chad called for him, beckoning him to the water. He had to do better at controlling his desire and ignore this all-consuming physical reaction anytime Chad was around. If not, he'd ruin everything between them.

"Get your ass in here!"

He was shit to do anything more than start down the ramp toward Chad.

"There's no way we're going to eat and drink all this," Ducky said, watching Chad add a variety of tropical fruits to the buggy already overfilled with a solid bottom layer of every kind of beer, wine, and liquor available in the store. The middle layer contained meat. Chicken, beef, pork, and fish. The top had a variety of vegetables and fruits balanced precariously. Chad handpicked every item with care, proclaiming his love of food and apparent love of cooking. Who knew Chad was a master griller in addition to all his other great qualities?

"See? Smell this right here." Chad extended a melon over the cart toward Ducky's nose. "I bet it's perfect. You can smell the sweetness."

Ducky hid the grin and leaned in. When his brow turned quizzical, only smelling the peel, Chad adjusted the melon.

He did in fact smell the ripeness. His brows lifted and he nodded. "Is that why you sniff around all these fruits?"

Chad placed the melon inside the basket and gathered two more as he answered. "Lots of 'em you can judge that way, but not all."

Chad tossed limes Ducky's way, laughing as Ducky scrambled to catch the airborne projectiles. He was ashamed to say several hit the floor because he was absolute shit at intercepting any of them.

"Papaya. Cool, here." A fruit the size of an oblong coconut was tossed at him next. He barely had it in his hands when Chad grabbed the end of the cart, and off they went toward the front of the store. His energy was boundless, always positive, and ready to get things done. Ducky trailed behind him, temporarily distracted by a shelf full of pre-baked cookies. It felt like forever since he tasted a cookie, and at the moment, the macadamia ones called to him.

A whistle caught his attention. Chad tossed a hand in the air, moving the groceries to a belt at checkout. "Those have carbs."

Carbs. How he loved carbs…

Ducky's grin was immediate. He grabbed two bags. The macadamia ones and another bag of a different flavor. For good measure, he grabbed a third one and started for Chad.

"Outside of the hamburger bun and french fries we ate, I haven't had a processed carb in months." He let the fruit and cookies drop onto the belt and grabbed a box of candy—looked like Skittles—and tossed them on the belt too. Maybe with a little more determination than necessary with the way Chad barked out a laugh.

"Do I need to rethink these meals?" Chad and the cashier stopped what they were doing, both looking blankly at him, waiting for his answer. The humor of the situation didn't go unnoticed. Ducky decided to add to the snacks. He grabbed two boxes of peanut M&M's and set them next to about half a dozen snickers that he'd knocked onto the belt with his free hand.

"No, keep going. I'm good."

"He's good," Chad parroted, turning back to the cashier. She gave a throaty laugh and continued to move items over the sensor, scanning the barcodes for the groceries.

"Seems so." She did that thing that both women and men alike did with Chad—take an instant like to him. He swore that Chad could draw a monk with a vow of silence into a lengthy conversation. He charmed everyone. "You two planning to set the island on fire?"

Chad gave an almost silent laugh and reached for his wallet. "I saw a brochure for a submarine scooter adventure. Recommend that?"

"Men like yourselves; I see you more as cage-free shark divers." Even though her tone was teasing, the alarm of such an adventure caught all of Ducky's attention.

"Where's that at? On the island?" Chad asked.

"Wait, what?" Ducky stepped in closer as Chad moved the cart around for the cashier to scan the drinks. Her cackle told him she'd hit her mark with the suggestion.

"I figure you're the daredevil." She nodded toward Chad. "And you're the quieter one. I suspect the more dangerous of the two…" She trailed off with a raised brow.

Now Chad barked out a loud laugh. "We should give shark diving a try."

Ducky refused to be swayed just in case Chad was serious. "Did you say cage-free? I feel like I'm out on that one. I'll watch from the boat, or I don't even have to go."

None of the humor had left Chad's face as he nodded and handed over his credit card to the cashier. Ducky was so lost in the sudden fear of diving into a school of sharks that he didn't even think to try to cover half the cost of their groceries. Shark diving. Oh man. Besides his always ready to plump cock, now he had to consider Chad's fearless athleticism.

He bet Chad could charm a great white shark into not biting him. Ducky, on the other hand, would be dinner, straight-up chum from the minute he hit the water.

CHAPTER 12
GRILL MASTER

The skills he'd learned camping with his father came in handy. Chad impressed himself by setting up a fire pit on the beach. He'd even used a rotisserie he'd found in the villa to grill their chicken for dinner. It worked out well enough, at least so far. Which was good since he'd made a big production of being the grill master for the trip.

Chad squatted down on his feet by the pit, balancing there as his toes dug into the sand. He rotated the corn on the cob lying on the outer edge of the rack. He had coated those with a good smattering of seasoned butter as he thought about all the showing off he'd been doing since seeing Ducky at the airport that morning.

Pretending to be into cage-free shark diving. He chuckled silently to himself. He was enough of a daredevil to follow through if Ducky had somehow wanted to go, but he also saw the value in keeping his appendages attached to his body.

"I brought paper plates," Ducky said, walking past Chad to the loungers they'd placed near the surf line.

They decided to chill tonight after Chad spent a couple of hours going through the masses of Wilder Sports emails. His and Ducky's plan was to take it easy and start fresh tomorrow morning to tackle everything the island had to offer. A drink cooler packed full of drinks sat between the loungers.

At the edge of the fire pit, Ducky's sandal-covered feet came into view. The crunching from above had Chad lifting his gaze, his hand pausing as he went back to turning the roasting meat. His grin was immediate. He saw a second run to the grocery store in their near future. Ducky was already on his second box of cookies since they'd made it back that afternoon.

"You know, this meal is better suited for a healthier diet."

Ducky quit chewing and stopped mid-motion with a cookie poised near his lips. He looked undecided if he wanted to take that bite or answer Chad. The latter won out, probably due to Ducky being a nice guy.

"I didn't know how badly I was craving snack food." The hand with the cookie continued its journey.

Chad shook his head at the sincerity of Ducky's expression. "Bring me your plate. These are ready."

Ducky did but only in the island pace he had adopted since the minute he landed in Hawaii. He took his role as vacationer to heart. There was no hurry. He went back for the plates and came forward again. Chad loaded each one with chicken and an assortment of the roasted vegetables. Ducky handed Chad his plate then circled around him to add a good portion of the seasoned butter he'd used while cooking the vegetables. He dumped most of it straight onto his plate before reaching over to offer the remaining for Chad's veggies.

"Want some?"

"No. I'd gain fifteen pounds if I ate all that," he teased.

Ducky only grinned and dumped the rest of the butter on his food. The box of cookies was lodged underneath his arm as he took his seat on the lounger. He sat on the side of the chair, scooting back enough to comfortably prop his feet on the edge of the cooler. The plate lay on his thighs as he dug into his food without any utensils.

"Did I tell you I hired a private chef at home?" Ducky asked, reaching for the napkins on the lounger, handing one to Chad when he took the seat across from Ducky.

Ducky's words stopped him from digging in, even though he was starving, and this was his kind of meal. They had glossed over Ducky hiring a personal chef while together at the restaurant back home.

"Like a person who comes to your apartment and prepares your food?"

Ducky nodded, lifting the chicken and taking a bite. It took a second for Ducky to answer. "This is good. You can cook."

"I told you I was good behind a grill," Chad said, taking his first bite. Ducky's praise had joy bubbling up inside him. "Tell me about this chef."

The reality of this moment, sitting casually on the tranquil beach, eating a simple meal as the sun slowly descended toward the horizon was soul-inspiring for Chad. Ducky's sweet nature and down-to-earth attitude sealed the deal for his heart. The way he plopped down and ate with his fingers, choosing to face Chad instead of the allure of the ocean… He really liked that move. There was no angling or pretense with Ducky. The alcohol they bought hadn't been touched.

These pockets of raw moments with Ducky left Chad feeling vulnerable in the best of ways. He wanted more. His heart stirred, fueling the connection between them.

"The chef was Greer's idea. He hired the guy for me to make healthy meals. He's in culinary school."

"That's cool. What did he say when he saw your apartment's kitchen for the first time?" Chad asked. Every personal chef he'd ever known had a thing about a proper kitchen to work within. He'd never been inside Ducky's apartment, but the buildings were older. He didn't see the kitchen being properly outfitted with fully modern equipment.

Ducky laughed, reaching for his water bottle, trying to avoid choking on the bite he'd just taken. "The guy walked in and looked around then asked me for my name again." The humor of the memory lit Ducky's handsome face. "I was given a list of things to buy before he could begin, and the guy still ended up preparing most of the food in his kitchen. I don't think he's pleased to be there. Greer told me he complains."

"No way you aren't throwing down some Big Mac's at two in the morning," Chad teased, trying his best to hide his own smile. He took the leap into the side of the transformation he had steered clear of. "What really made you do all this to yourself?"

The hilarity of the previous moment slipped off Ducky as he turned away from Chad to stare out at the ocean. His friend waited so long to answer, Chad thought he'd broached a subject that was meant to be off limits.

"Forget it, you don't have to answer. You didn't tell any of us what you were doing. It was really a shock. I've decided it was the hair. I'm not sure I've ever seen your eyes before."

The inner struggle that took Ducky's attention vanished. "I didn't want to cut my hair, but it seemed like the right thing to do once I started with the new clothes. I don't know..." Ducky said the puzzling words and took another bite from his plate. He reached for his napkin, running it over his mouth then wiping the greasy butter off his fingertips. "I'm in a weird place. I don't know who I am anymore. I thought the clothes were going to make me feel different."

Ducky's troubled gaze settled on Chad with a look he'd seen several times since they'd had their first face-to-face meeting days ago. An expression that finally had a reason that Chad didn't fully understand.

"What do you mean?" he asked, reaching for the napkin, completely ignoring the plate of food in his lap.

"Everything's different now." Ducky took another bite, chewing without the gusto he'd eaten with before. "You and Kai are the only people in my life that treat me the same as you used to. But I think that's my fault, not theirs. I'm different. I thought changing my outside appearance would help my inside catch up." Ducky tapped his temple to indicate the change was in his head. "It didn't though. What I thought I wanted didn't fill this void inside like I thought it would."

"Keep explaining," Chad encouraged.

"I don't know what I mean. It's like I've got all this money, but I have no idea who I am anymore." Chad held the full weight of Ducky's stare. "Do you get what I mean?"

"Maybe," Chad said, sensing they were both in this weird self-discovery stage. "I've been going through something too. The thing I wanted isn't the thing I wanted after all.

Everything's changed."

"Yeah, that's it," Ducky said, his eyes growing wide in some sort of shared understanding. "When StreamTrainer was barely making it, I worked all the time, but life was normal. I never had much so it didn't matter that I didn't have much. When we started making money, I kept socking it away, trying to ignore it because the business was growing so quickly. Now we have a large staff, and everyone seems to know their place, except me."

Chad nodded, hoping to follow along. "As if the money was supposed to make you happy and complete, but it didn't."

"Right." Ducky nodded, putting the plate aside. He leaned forward, grabbing his knees with his arms in that protective way he had when crossing his arms over his chest. "I realized that I was the one who changed. I'm different."

"Me too. I'm changed."

They stared at one another, sharing an understanding in their silent exchange.

"What're you moving away from?" Ducky asked.

"Golf." Chad didn't hesitate in telling his truth. "I feel like the decision's made. I haven't picked up a club in weeks. No desire to. Did I tell you about the offer Tristan made me?"

"No," Ducky said, giving his full attention to Chad as if nothing else in the world mattered.

"He made me an offer to head up Wilder Sports. It's a significant position under Wilder, Inc."

Ducky's brows lifted in surprise. "What would you have to do?"

"I'd be the lead over the whole program. Do it all. I'd have a senior vice president title in Wilder. I'd have staff to find talent, approve negotiations, control budgets… The salary is big. The whole thing. Tristan shocked me when he made the offer. I figured he'd ask me to work for him to find athletes, but I never expected a senior role. I was just shown the contract seconds before you came on the screen. I was already stunned when I looked up and saw you. I didn't mean…" Chad found himself apologizing to Ducky again.

"How does it feel to get such an offer?" Ducky asked, stopping Chad before he started tripping over himself in another drawn out explanation of his inadvertently tactless remark. A good call on Ducky's part.

Chad hadn't let himself consider the offer in that way. When he let his thoughts shift that direction, the anxiety building at having to make such a decision eased off. "Honestly, I worry it'll be seen as a nepotism issue and not based on my value to the company. But then I also see where I'd be a really good fit. I'll work hard and earn my position. Part of my struggle with golf is that I'm finding I want to use my education. I have a strong business sense. I want to pair that with sports."

The frown between Ducky's brows faded. "You'd come in clutch in that position, no lie. You always make things happen. I've never known anyone as motivated as you are, but you also get bored easily when you're stuck in one place. I think if you had a job where you got to move around, travel, be on the road, you'd be into that."

Chad nodded, agreeing. He appreciated the depth in which Ducky truly understood him. "Yeah, I get antsy pretty easily."

"I never said anything, but I never saw golf as your thing. You're an extrovert with control issues." Ducky's grin spread wide as he lifted the box of cookies and dug in.

"Hey now." Chad scoffed as if offended but didn't disagree. He couldn't. He knew he liked to manage his world. "So let me ask you what you asked me. How does it feel to hit the big time?"

Ducky's shoulder slumped ever so subtly as if something inside Ducky wilted. He finished chewing his bite. The box was discarded by the plate.

"I don't know how it feels. I can't figure it out. Having all this success isn't anything I've ever wanted, you know? Like…" Ducky blew out a breath. "I don't know. I think I should buy a house. I don't know where though. Maybe in Greer's development in Washington State," Ducky said, then stopped speaking. The line between his brows deepened, showing exactly how bothered Ducky was by everything changing around him. "Full confession?"

"Sure. I've got you, you know that," Chad promised, sitting up a little straighter, taking Ducky's words as seriously as he'd ever taken anything.

"I don't like having all this money. I think that's my problem," Ducky answered. It was Chad's turn to give Ducky a confused, concerned look. He never heard anyone say something like that before. "It's changed everything. My friends treat me differently. There's a huge divide in my family. I haven't talked to my brother Donny or my father for years now. And on top of all that, you know I fundamentally believe 'the man' is a greedy bastard, and I'm afraid I've become no better or I'm headed that direction."

"Your brother's an asshole. Who cares if you haven't spoken to him?" Chad could physically see Ducky drawing into himself. "I've been going through it too. When my father came out and partnered with Tristan, I lost a lot of my identity. No matter where I am or what I accomplish, I'm always reduced to the son of one of the wealthiest power couples in the world. I can't figure out how to get myself back. Do you think we're going through some kind of twenty-something crisis?" The question was as serious as anything he'd ever asked before.

"Maybe that's it." Ducky turned on the lounger, placing his plate on the sand beside his chair. He drew his legs up, again holding them with his arms. All the muscle and tight cords ran the length of both Ducky's legs, threatening to derail Chad's focus. "Maybe I want to give the money away. Is that dumb? Am I too young to make a decision like that?"

It seemed an extreme idea. Certainly, one he'd never heard anyone suggest before. "What about investing it? You never know what's going to happen to StreamTrainer."

"Except I kind of do," Ducky explained. "We have all these focus groups going all the time. The new row machine and upgrade to the mirror are projected to hit big this fall. Greer was a genius to start selling the fitness boxes to corporations. Then Dallas started competitions between companies. The data coming in is already showing a fitter employee base for those on the corporate level. That means insurance wellness programs are interested. At this point, we could give the boxes away and still make money on the monthly fees. Greer keeps turning down offers to buy us full out. It's insane."

"What about giving Greer your money to invest in the nonprofits he funds," Chad asked, not fully able to absorb the amounts of money Ducky must be talking about.

"That's where all my cash is now. He's handling it. Now my money is making money."

"Is that where the motivation to change your appearance came from? Like you wanted to look like someone with all that money? Did you really go to Greer, or did he come to you?" Chad asked, not liking anything he was hearing. Why change the most genuinely good person he had ever known?

"I went to him, but Greer doesn't do anything halfway. I don't know how Dallas stood a chance against him. They have this life that looks like something I want." Ducky's jaw set tighter. His unsettled gaze cast out over the ocean, lost there. "After the last six months, I'm not so much there anymore. It's hard. Working out, watching your diet, dressing a certain way is a lot to undertake. Add in the constant work of my job and it's all I had time for." He ran his fingers through his short strands. "Cutting my hair was the biggest deal for me. I felt exposed and it's so straight. How did they get it this straight?"

"It had to be black magic." The tease worked. Ducky turned a grin toward Chad and rolled his eyes. "I always liked your hair the other way too. It was a mess of curls." He matched Ducky's grin as he lifted his hands above his head to represent the height and reach those curls could go.

"You're a dork." Ducky wadded his napkin, tossing it toward Chad. "Stop making fun of me."

"I'm not at all," Chad said, easily catching the napkin and tossing it back at Ducky. This time, he reached for the cooler sitting between them. Aggravation replaced his good mood as he spotted a group of people walking toward them. "We have company headed our way."

Ducky glanced over his shoulder to where five bathing suit clad women were walking down the beach toward them.

"Let's make a deal. No more serious stuff until it's time to go home. We'll make our decisions with a rested outlook on life," Chad said, caught between relief and frustration at having other people around. He and Ducky fit so well together which only enhanced the crush Chad had on his friend. But that only added to the annoyance of losing their alone time to these women.

"Seems fair enough," Ducky replied, getting to his feet. He picked up both their plates, and other trash, then started for the villa.

"Where're you going?" Chad asked, twisting a top off the beer he'd lifted from the cooler. "They're almost here."

"I gotta pee. You do your thing. I'll be back."
Chad had no idea if that was the truth or nerves on Ducky's part. Either way, he didn't have time to do anything more than get to his feet as the ladies invaded their space.

CHAPTER 13
HAWAII

Chad sure had a way of drawing people to him. They hadn't been settled in their villa for more than twelve hours and people, both vacationers and locals, were sprinkled throughout the kitchen, living room, and flowing onto the back lanai. Ducky casually strolled through the house like a teenager's parent, keeping an eye on his things. He'd brought about five thousand dollars' worth of technology with him on this trip. He didn't want it to walk off.

He sipped on his third beer of the night, listening to The Pretty Reckless belt out their hard-edged sounds, nodding in time with the headbanger tempo. Shockingly, he hadn't felt out of place with all the toned, barely clad bodies everywhere. He stepped outside, the music following as he went, and stood watching the dark waves of the ocean crash into the shoreline as he lifted his bottle for another drink.

"Duck, over here," Chad called out. His friend sat on the L-shaped outdoor furniture, two of the original four women lounged next to him. Ducky suspected their large supply of alcohol, only purchased a few hours ago, would need to be replenished tomorrow. "I was telling them about your newest modeling campaign."

He barely held back the burst of laughter as he walked toward Chad. The attention of everyone in the vicinity landed on him as if they were trying to place him as a celebrity. Ducky made the mental note to get Chad back for that one. He did what he had done all evening: stayed silent as he positioned himself on the edge of the hard wicker furniture.

"What agency are you with?" Felicia asked, angling toward Ducky which meant she had to release the hold she had around Chad's shoulders. Her forearm landed on Ducky's thigh as she leaned forward. "I'm with IMG agency out of New York."

Ducky nodded and lifted his brows, staring down at the sun-kissed blonde giving off all the interested vibes. Felicia was clearly tipsy. The way her bikini top barely covered her breasts, he'd guess it wouldn't take much to get her out of it. He'd never had anyone who looked like her interested in him before. Why did this add another layer to the superficial life he wanted no part of?

She waited, looking adoringly at him as if he held all the secrets to the world. Ducky lifted his gaze to Chad who was clearly having the time of his life at his expense, like only a longtime friend might do.

The nerves hit hard. On the regular, he had no interest in small talk but for Chad he would try.

"Agency for what?" Ducky asked, lifting the bottle for a longer drink.

"Modeling agency." She slapped his leg playfully as if he were the silliest guy on the planet.

"No agency. Only a very frustrating executive team." He crossed a single arm over his chest because he didn't know what to do with it. The arm felt awkward hanging between his body and hers. The confusion staring at him by Felicia and her friends had Chad nodding, motioning his head as if Ducky were expected to say more.

"What executive team? What does he mean?" the woman sitting on the other side of Chad asked.

"He's part owner of StreamTrainer. The workout—" Chad started and was immediately cut off.

"I work out on StreamTrainer all the time. My brother got me hooked on it. I knew I knew you. I just took a class with you and Skye… Skye, right?" She left Chad's side, stepping over him to move closer to Ducky. Felicia wasn't having any of it. She scooted fully against Ducky's side. "You're Duncan Reigns but they call you Ducky. I'm Ava. Felicia and I've been friends forever."

Heat whooshed up his cheeks with the intensity of a wildfire spreading over dry forest land. His gaze landed on Chad who burst out laughing at his obvious discomfort. The entire mood changed in the small group. Chad was no longer the sole focus of their attention, and he seemed fine with it. So much so that he got to his feet and slid past Ducky's adoring audience.

"You won an award, right?" Ava continued.

Based on Felicia's bristled expression, she didn't like Ava's sudden interest. Chad chuckled that much more. The weight of Chad's hand clamped on Ducky's shoulder, giving a gentle, teasing squeeze. He didn't immediately remove his palm. It lingered. His fingertips touching the bare skin of Ducky's neck. Ducky's heart fluttered at the innocent skin to skin contact. The warmth from his face coasted all over his body. His eyes slid shut involuntarily, his mouth watering as Chad leaned in. That scent of spicy musk assailed Ducky, plumping his cock. Chad's lips were so close to Ducky's ear he could feel them part. Chad's quick intake of breath sent tingles racing along his arms, tiny bumps followed their path.

"Wingman and such." The following low-level chuckle sent puffs of Chad's warm breath coating his skin. For the briefest of moments, nothing more than he and Chad existed in the world. Ducky tucked his chin to his chest, relishing the sudden quiet of all the chaos in his life. An alternate universe prevailed, one where someone like Chad wanted someone like him. He imagined they were friends, lovers, and partners in the craziness of the world. Ducky's heart slowed as the vision firmed in his mind. He saw the world so clearly.

Chad lifted his head, his hand followed, and the magic of the moment dissipated. The clear image turned into a haze of smoke until the last wisp vanished. Then the chaos snapped back into his head. The peace was lost to reality. Even the relaxation of a new vacation didn't remain as Felicia took notice of his rigid length. The purr in her voice spoke of all the things she was willing to do with him.

"I bet you do very well for yourself, don't you?"

Back on the new playing field of his life, he understood the calculation darkening her eyes. The entirety of his existence became dollar signs. Ducky tried his best to ignore Felicia and took a drink of his lukewarm beer. Ava tapped away on her phone until she found his most recent workout video on StreamTrainer and turned the phone's screen to show those surrounding them.

"I've gotta pee," he said. Heat suffused his cheeks as the camera focused on him. It still took several long moments to untangle himself from the group.

He had nowhere to escape to in the packed house, so he went to his bedroom for as much solitude as he could muster. He hadn't checked on StreamTrainer all day. If nothing else, email was going to be a bitch to get through.

Chad sat at the kitchen bar, drinking a cup of coffee. One eye on Ducky's closed door, the other on his cell phone as he searched the local attractions. Their itinerary sat to the side. He used bits and pieces of Dallas's suggestions for excursions. Many had already been prepaid. Ducky only had to call and set up times.

The list of activities included hiking, biking, parasailing, and surfing. Also boating, skiing, and snorkeling. All included introductory lessons, and none seemed like anything he'd ever known Ducky to like to do.

Perhaps more had changed than just Ducky's outer shell.

Chad's full gaze cut to Ducky's bedroom door again. More than anything, he wanted that door to open.

Yeah, right. More than anything, he wanted Ducky to be in there alone.

He again ticked off the chicks he recalled from the party. The best he remembered, they'd all left the villa, but Ducky's door had been shut for a good long time.

Focus. He looked back down at his cell phone. The screen had timed out. He didn't even remember what he'd been reading before.

He swiveled around on the barstool toward the long windows overlooking the beach. He intended to jog off his frustrations this morning. After a fitful night, waking early to greet the rising sun seemed symbolic of shedding all this nervous energy reverberating through him. Now, two and a half hours later, he sat on this stool, his leg bouncing on the bottom rung, hyped up on his third cup of coffee. His foot picked up the bouncing as if to prove the point. His gaze slid to Ducky's door again.

Why had he agreed to come to Hawaii? He hung his head and turned back toward the kitchen. Because Ducky's happiness was steadily becoming the most important thing to him. That was the only reason he'd engaged with those superficial women in the first place. Ducky was down and confused with himself. If he had the ability to help ease some of his burden, then he was compelled to.

Same thought applied to all these island activities. If Ducky had changed into a guy who liked to try new sports, then he was the person to help teach Duck. He and his father had tackled all these adventures at various points in his life.

He scratched his naked belly and ran his hand through his disheveled hair. With as many times as he'd executed this same move, the thick strands surely had to be standing on end. He brought his phone back to life, reading the same paragraph for the third time now. The private surfing lessons had availability in a couple of hours then again at that same time every day.

Ducky's door creaked open. Chad tensed from head to toe. He had to steel his resolve to look over at Ducky. That betraying reaction, the one he'd had during the podcast, lit his body on fire as he stared openly at the man in the doorway. His short athletic shorts hung low on his hips. They were the only thing Ducky wore, which wasn't much different from what Chad was wearing.

The sexually charged moment had Chad ducking his head, peeking at his lap, praying he hadn't tented his shorts. He was stone hard, but partially hidden by his underwear. Something so rigid he'd have to rub one off in the very near future.

How the hell could he get through the next thirteen days like this?

Only then did he remember that Ducky might have a bed partner. His gaze shifted behind the object of his desire. Maybe that would be the only thing to tame his visceral reaction. No one followed Ducky out.

"Morning," Ducky said, his voice deep, thick, and sexy as he scratched the top of his head.

"Morn—" Chad started with a croak and had to clear his throat as he feigned interest in the itinerary and his now darkened phone screen. "Morning. You have a good night?"

Ducky headed toward the coffee pot and let go of a long, jaw-popping yawn. His hand went to his head again. Nothing was a confidence destroyer like knowing he was the only one sexually amped up like this.

"I stayed up working." Another yawn stopped him midsentence.

Chad's unabashed gaze slid to Ducky, all pretense of doing anything more was impossible. He soaked in Ducky's rumpled, sleepy appearance. "I thought you'd be in there with one of those chicks."

Ducky's green stare pinned him in place when he looked at him over his shoulder. Ducky was in the middle of starting the Keurig but stopped just shy of pressing the brew button. Confusion showed on his face, which in turn confused Chad too.

"What are you talking about?" Ducky asked, the

uncertainty still etched on his face.

"Those women you were talking to. I thought the blonde and brunette were going to throw down over you," Chad answered, one side of his lips quirking in a smile.

Ducky's head shook. Not necessarily a no, more like Chad was ridiculous then dismissed. Ducky focused all his attention on the coffee maker. That was all right. Chad mapped every inch of the broad shoulders leading to the muscles running down toward the trim waist. Ducky's shorts hung so low he could see the two dimples right above his ass. His mouth watered with a desire to nibble on that toned flesh.

Ducky turned toward him again. He clamped his eyes closed, the sweep of Ducky's strong back and tight ass etched in vivid detail behind the darkness of his lids. When he reluctantly opened his eyes, Ducky stood directly across from him on the opposite side of the bar. Steam rose from the coffee cup sitting between them. Ducky seemed unaffected by the chemistry they shared, a bond Chad felt deep inside his veins. His friend's elbows landed on the counter as he rubbed his hands down the length of his face and gave a jaw-cracking yawn again.

"Those people last night were weird. I ditched them a few minutes after you left. I swear I saw dollar signs in the blonde's eyes."

Chad chuckled, and forced his attention down to his phone, wanting coherent conversation to replace the rambling jumble of his thoughts.

"Did you end up with any of them?" Ducky asked.

"No way. I kicked everybody out at two. I thought you'd hooked up and gone to bed, but I was too tired. I sort of picked up the mess then crashed." His hand shot over his shoulder toward the living room, veranda, and beach. "I got the bottles and cans up. That's about it."

"There's a housekeeper included," Ducky reminded him, lifting his coffee cup to take a small sip. "What're you doing?" he asked with a nod toward Chad's cell.

Chad let out a sigh and stopped pretending to do anything more than drink Ducky in. "We can hit this private lesson for surfing if you want. If we go now, we could get a bite to eat before the lesson."

"Surfing," Ducky said, showing no emotion or physical cue to let Chad know what he thought. "Do you want to?"

"If you do." A moment of apparent indecision happened before Ducky pushed off the counter, his cup in hand, and started back for his bedroom.

"Yeah. Let's go."

CHAPTER 14
I WIN

Three days later

The sun beat down on Ducky, the warmth already drying his wet skin as he pulled himself from the water. Today's activity came by way of a hike. A place Chad found. One point nine miles that ended in a waterfall. The cliffs of the lush green mountain range were the perfect angles to dive from. Swimming under the falls added to the tranquility. Nature's natural rhythmic meditation filled his soul with calm.

The peace he'd found in all these outdoor activities Chad kept dragging him to had begun to fill the void inside him. Ducky could breathe here. His crowded thoughts disappeared. How had he never known how much he enjoyed outdoor physical activity?

Instead of getting lost on any one problem, Ducky dropped his T-shirt on the rock and lay back on the small edge of the cliff, closing his eyes against the sun.

"Pale skin needs sunscreen," Chad called from the water and expertly clapped a splash of water, sending the spray over Ducky's entire body. He didn't even care or budge a single muscle. All he could do was grin. His fair skin had been a source of teasing since the first time they went surfing, and he had regularly sprayed his exposed skin with sunscreen.

Little did he know such a natural safety precaution could result in days of ridicule. Chad beat his brothers in the expert level of dishing out trash talk. The two of them were becoming as close as brothers.

Something anxiety-filled rejected the notion. He shoved those feelings aside, deciding days ago he'd take what he could get from Chad. He owed Chad. More now than any other time before. This trip gave him a sense of normalcy. A new normal, allowing for the experiences and growth he'd had over the last few years while still really feeling at peace with himself.

He lifted his arm, raising his middle finger to Chad by way of an answer. Chad's bark of laughter had Ducky's grin growing wider. The larger splash of water that came next was Chad's answer to his crude action. What he didn't expect was Chad's burst from the water, using the ledge to pull himself up. Dripping water spilled across the rocky edge, saturating Ducky. He ducked out of the way while throwing out a hand, knocking Chad's hard chest. The hit was just enough to have Chad lose his hold on the edge and fall back into the water.

The resulting *oomph* had Ducky instantly looking over the side to see for himself as Chad hit the water with a hard splash.

He didn't know his own strength and wanted to high five himself for such a great move.

"Hey," Chad said, spitting and sputtering once his head popped up from the water. Another hand splash followed, this one with more force. Ducky could only assume Chad was master-level skilled at sending the most amount of water splashing forward with the least amount of hand effort.

The retaliation came so fast with such force it caught Ducky off guard. A wave of water landed in his open eyes, the force pushing him backward. He landed on his ass and back as Chad leaped up, easily climbing the ledge to stand over Ducky. All the water cascading off him in pools, landed on Ducky, soaking him and all their belongings through.

"Your shoes are wet. It's gonna suck to walk back in those," Chad teased in a menacing tone. Ducky barely held on to his urge to shove Chad off the ledge again. Instead, he lay back as if he didn't have a care in the world, closing his eyes. Even tossing a dismissive arm over his eyes for good measure.

"Those are your shoes. Mine are on the ledge above." Ducky tried to hide his smile—Lord knew he did—but he couldn't hold the indifference. He grinned, completely unprepared for Chad's next move. He felt the sprinkle of water before Chad's body came down on top of his. Wet, hard, and dominating. Chad pinned him down like a pro. A move Ducky had no question came from WWE. Chad straddled his waist and jerked both his hands above his head, shaking his wet hair and upper chest into Ducky's face.

Instinctually, Ducky's body hardened and hummed. His cock grew stiff in seconds flat. All he could do was squint against the sun, hoping to dispel the droplets while still taking in everything about this moment. This was what it would look like to have Chad moving over him.

His chest heaved, finding it hard to catch his breath. He

had to fight the urge to lift his hips and rut against his best friend. Chad's weight above him, pressing him down felt too good.

"Give. I win," Chad goaded.

The longing in his heart finally subsided enough to let oxygen enter his lungs. Lucky, since his vision had started to blur. His hopes collided with reality.

What the fuck was happening? Of course, he didn't try to fight Chad. Not until Chad shifted slightly, coming within inches of his rigid cock. Fear made him panic. How could Chad understand his hard-on?

The anxiety of ruining their friendship gave Ducky more strength than he ever thought possible. He busted a move, easily dislodging Chad's hold on his hands while causing him to fall forward. Chad's chest fell into his face. The skin to skin contact set the neurons in his brain into overdrive. But Chad wasn't the only one who'd religiously watched WWE in his youth. Ducky called forward his John Cena days. He had to move Chad off him without hurting either one of them.

Ducky spun. Chad's now-wet towel cushioned the fall. Chad's muscular legs locked around his waist as he changed their position and looked down on his friend. Fuck, this angle wasn't any better.

Challenge lit in those blue eyes. Both Chad's arms circled his chest, tightening in a death grip.

What the hell was he doing? The awkward position had him inches from Chad's handsome face. His eyes bored into Ducky. The gaze sent a sizzle ricocheting from his heart to his head, promising things Ducky didn't understand.

Chad's full lips were so close and tempting. What would happen if he leaned in and pressed his mouth against Chad's?

Fuck. Ducky started to loosen his hold. The need to put distance between himself and Chad overwhelmed his senses. Longing had to be reflected in his gaze. One breath then another as they continued to stare at each other.

Ducky had it so damn bad. He was losing the battle raging in his soul.

Did friendship really matter that much? He dipped his head.

Chad took the advantage Ducky gave. "You think you're the only one with moves?"

He gave a wicked laugh and pushed them both off the side of the ledge. They landed with a hard splash into the water only a few feet away. Chad didn't let him go as they went under, not until they sank as low as they could go. Then his friend pushed them both to the surface, still holding Ducky tightly.

Being completely unprepared for the spontaneous submersion, Ducky spit and coughed out the water he'd taken in.

Chad gave a boisterous laugh right in Ducky's face "I win."

Ducky planted both hands on Chad's chest and shoved away, using his feet against Chad's body as a launching point. He swam a few feet away unsure how Chad could have missed his hard cock, but the threat of drowning had dimmed his arousal. He swam in place, looking at Chad's shit-eating grin.

"I still win," Chad said.

"You keep saying that," Ducky shot back, not yet ready to give in on the fight. Chad's response was to swim toward Ducky with determination in his eyes. "Okay, okay. You win. I lost. Is that what you want?" Ducky managed to stop Chad about half a foot away.

"I want your shoes for the walk back as my prize."

Ducky rolled his eyes and performed his own slap to the water, sending a wave over Chad's face before swimming the long way around to the ledge.

"Screw that," he said and lifted himself out of the water with his back turned to Chad. He kept climbing to reach his joggers before Chad could get them. "You can walk barefoot."

Chad had forgotten how much he loved to spend time in the kitchen. Five days into their vacation and he constantly gravitated to the heart of the home, forgoing the local restaurants, preparing his and Ducky's meals himself. The great thing about feeding Ducky was that he happily ate whatever Chad made. Even seemed appreciative of his efforts.

The other great thing was that Ducky never complained about how often they went to the grocery store. They vibed so well together. The atmosphere they lived in was chill and relaxed to say the least. They meshed well. Ducky was one of the most considerate, well-intentioned people Chad had ever known. The guy was sweet, personable, and real. The last attribute was exactly what Chad had needed to help ground him with his recent turbulent thoughts.

No matter what, Ducky needed to stay in the forefront of his immediate circle. The way Ducky helped him unplug from the chaos in his head made decision-making so much easier. On that thought, he put the knife down and reached for a cloth towel to wipe his hands from the vegetables he'd been chopping.

In a move he'd never been more sure of in his life, a peace settled over him as he pulled up Tristan's contact information and sent him a text message.

"I'd like to formally accept the position. I have the e-copy of the contract. I'll sign it and send it to Human Resources in the morning."

Chad looked out past the lanai, down to the beach where Ducky sat alone, meditating, or so he explained his actions in that way. It seemed a stretch to think the tension still lingering around Ducky could be solely healed by meditation, but he hoped he had given Ducky the same support he'd gotten in return.

A driving certainty had him glancing back down to his cell to finish the message. *"I'm going to pull back from the PGA. I'm not feeling it at all anymore. I'm thankful for everything you and Dad did to help me achieve my goals. I hope my dad won't be too disappointed with me."*

After all the self-reflection, his father's disappointment was his only true regret. He pushed send, glanced back at Ducky still on the beach, staring into the deep blue water then took the coward's way out, swiftly typing another message to Tristan. *"Can you tell Dad for me?"*

The little boy in him nervously waiting for his father's approval was a damn hard feeling to shake. Having his father pleased with him fed a deeper insecurity. Yet he'd never remembered a time his dad hadn't offered him everything.

Tristan's text came back quickly. *"I think it's a good decision for you and the company. I'll instruct HR to expedite your new-hire paperwork. I watched the video of the cliff diver you're interested in from Italy. She's crazy talented. I want you to go scout her, but as a father figure to you, I don't want you to go fling yourself off those high cliffs like I know you might."*

Of course, he was eventually going to try cliff diving. Those athletes were too talented to not try to glean perspective. His thoughts scattered and any comeback was lost when his father's name appeared on his screen. His ring tone, specifically the vibrant, loud *woo hoo* chorus from "Song 2" by Blur, always grabbed all the attention no matter where he was.

All the certainty from moments ago became unsteady. He hadn't anticipated having to have this call so fast. On the fourth ring, Chad answered, "Hey."

"Hey," his father repeated. "Tristan forwarded me your text. Is this truly the decision you want to make? Everyone has second thoughts and down times. You'll build back, Chad—"

"It's what I want, Dad," Chad said firmly. He closed his eyes as the conviction resurrected in full force. "I want this. I've already started fielding talent. I don't like being tied to one sport. This is a way I can use my education and still be a part of an industry I love. Unless you don't think I'm qualified for such a big job." He took a gulp of a breath, sensing he was rambling, and waited for his father's answer.

"You know I believe you can handle the job," his dad said easily. "It'll take a lot from you, but I agree with Tristan. You're ready to find your purpose. I was your age when I started watching Six Degrees and Xanga. If I hadn't tried to put the two together into a more interactive social site, Secret would have never happened. You have to remember, your strength is also your weakness. You're young, smart, and motivated. Once you channel all your energy into a career, the world will open for you like never before. I've said all this before."

Chad had to resist the urge to roll his eyes only because, yes, he'd heard all these things his whole life. "Dad, I've thought long and hard about this. It's part of the reason I took some time off to really consider everything."

"You're in Hawaii with Ducky?" Dylan asked. "Chloe told me."

Of course, she did. Always in everyone's business. "I am. I've started cooking again. I'm enjoying it." That reminded Chad of the chicken on the stove, and he turned to tend the sizzling meat he'd forgotten once he'd texted Tristan. "I have to go. I'm right in the middle of cooking dinner."

"For you and Ducky?" Dylan asked, his voice betraying nothing beyond that simple question.

Who else would it be for? He even shook his head at the empty room. "Yeah. I'll call you later. Dinner's burning. Bye." Chad pushed end to the call. He tossed his phone on the counter, rolled his eyes as he grabbed the tongs to turn the chicken breasts to the other side. Maybe his next mental health issue to tackle will be his daddy issues. He was a grown ass man who acted like a child every time he spoke to his father.

Anderson .Paak played at high volume from Chad's open bedroom door. Even though they had completely different tastes in music, Ducky dropped down on the sofa, elbows on his knees with phone in hand, bobbing his head to the addicting beat. Tonight, the party wasn't happening at their place. Instead, everyone planned to go to a nightclub, one the locals hung out in.

Much like every day of his life, he had no idea what to wear and decided on something between casual and formal, and Greer inspired, darker blue slacks, a violet button down with the shirt sleeves rolled up to right below his elbows, and tan loafers. The way the clothes fit, he might be cutting off circulation to his hands.

The joke made him laugh because there was probably some truth to the thought.

Really none of it mattered more than the glaring fact that his ad campaign had gone live that afternoon. Not just live, but on blast. His images were littered all over the place, both social and online media as well as billboards. As someone who thought Tom from Myspace was brilliant to follow all his members' pages, Ducky had arranged to do the same on StreamTrainer's social site. He kept getting dinged over and over each time a picture of a billboard starring his barely clad before and after pictures were posted.

Based on his level ten annoyance factor, he clearly hadn't gotten over his anger of this campaign being allowed to go live. They shouldn't have gone around him like they had. Maybe they could have given him a minute to get comfortable with the idea. Partnership sucked.

"Hey, you're ready," Chad said, causing Ducky to lift his thumbs from his cell phone and look up. Chad's steps faltered until he came to a stop, his focused gaze zoomed in on Ducky, his brow furrowed. Ducky's mouth dropped open. Chad had mimicked his look, pressed pants, dress shirt, all made to fit. Chad wore it so much better. He had an effortless chic that made him captivating. From the perfect sweep of his dark hair to the deep tan and light-colored eyes. He swore to God his cock just went on strike, refusing to settle down ever again. He ended up standing for comfort. "You look hot."

If only that were true, or maybe better said, if only Chad meant it in a way that Ducky wanted. He started to speak and had to clear his throat and mind to help sound less like a fool.

As he'd done a thousand times already, he wondered why he'd ever thought bringing Chad along was a good idea. He had it so bad that Chad walking in a room caused Ducky's desire to freak the fuck out. This was Dallas's fault too. Between his brother's frustrating strong-arm tactics, his huge lack of sleep that day, and being stunned that Chad was standing in front of him at the office, Ducky pretended like this was the best idea ever. It wasn't.

Finally, the signals connected in his head. Ducky didn't say anything he truly wanted to, instead he murmured, "You don't think I'm overdressed?"

He concentrated on turning off his phone and pushing a hand inside his front pocket. Eyes focused on the center of Chad's chest.

"We're dressed exactly the same," Chad said and looked down the length of his clothes.

His eyes had a mind of their own and followed Chad's lead, mapping the hard body. Where Ducky's cock was firm and solid, Chad's was flaccid, the big downer to the otherwise slowly tanking mood.

He blew out a breath and patted his back pockets to ensure his wallet was there. He cut his gaze away. With the hours he'd spent on the beach, staring at the ocean, meditating heavily over his current life choices, thoughts of Chad played like a chanting anthem, derailing all his effort to pull his life together.

He liked Chad, even more now that he saw what a

genuinely caring guy he was. His down-to-earth decency created a burden of its own. Somehow, this trip had added new layers of complication for him.

Today had been a turning point. He'd made decisions while sitting alone in the sand. First, and most important, he would become a person worthy of someone like Chad. He did want a good relationship like Dallas and Greer had. Someone to love him and accept his love in return. He wanted to be with a man. Honestly, women had never felt right. He'd only dated women because his father had been such a dick to Dallas over his sexuality. But his unrelenting sexual dreams held blue eyes, a nice covering of beard, and a hard cock.

"What's the look for?" Chad asked.

Ducky shook his thoughts clear and made it to the front door. He pulled the door open and looked back over his shoulder, refusing to make eye contact with Chad.

"Are we leaving?" Ducky asked. He'd gotten lost in his head again and needed to stay present. "The Uber's here."

Chad's response was a low chuckle as he dropped his shoes on the floor, edging them onto his bare feet. "All right." He clapped his hands and moved to an unheard beat, dancing out the door ahead of Ducky. "We're going out. Let's get this party started."

Ducky nearly groaned at the sensual grind of those hips with each step Chad took. The motion threatened to throw Ducky right back into that fantasy world, imagining possibilities.

.

CHAPTER 15
LET'S DANCE

At home, Ducky would have never voluntarily picked a nightclub like this to hang out in. Man, he'd been wrong not to try one before now. He had no idea the name of the band, but he liked the way the sexy remix made him feel. The music played like an anthem to the dancers on the dance floor gyrating around him. Hell, he'd never even heard the hypnotic sounds before, but it didn't matter, he'd still shake his ass around the lighted dance floor.

Drinks flowed as if cash didn't matter. Even after pacing himself, Ducky's head swam. He'd long past gotten over the embarrassment of the advertising campaign releasing today, literally every single patron of the bar had seen him on the Secret mobile app.

Well, the real reason for that was Felicia. When he and Chad had first walked in, Felicia had become the bar crier, showing everyone, from the locals to the tourists alike, the ad campaign with his almost nude before and after pictures. He'd gone from nobody to bar favorite in under a minute, having to meet and talk to more people than he had for the entirety of the trip. Maybe that was why he'd started hanging out on the dance floor, drinking more than he should.

He found acceptance in this crowd, something he'd never experienced before. He wasn't the odd man out, the misunderstood one, sitting on the outskirts of life. He'd always wondered what it felt like to be on the inside, a normal one. These kinds of people weren't as superficial as he'd once thought. Only interested in how they looked, never going deeper with their thoughts on anything. He'd gotten it wrong in his assessments. Many were really good people.

He bounced his body to the beat, no real idea how to dance and had no partner. The best part was that he didn't have to ask anyone to dance. They were asking him. What a mind fuck. He couldn't remember a time in his life that anyone had ever asked him to dance.

"Here," Felicia said in his ear, coming from behind Ducky, moving slower than the song dictated. She lifted a cocktail glass for him.

"What is it?" Ducky called out, still dancing around in front of her.

"Ice water," she yelled back, pushing it into his hands. "Like you asked for. You're the hit of the club. Everybody's got you out dancing."

He chuckled, slowing down until he stood in the middle of the floor next to her. He took the drink, lifting the glass to down the contents in a couple of hearty gulps. Like he'd done over and again for most of the night, he cast a quickish, sly glance toward Chad who sat at their high-top table, keeping anyone from trying to take their seats. A group of club goers—mostly the friends they had met and partied with every night—sat around him.

Charm exuded from Chad. His easy grin tripped Ducky's heart even if it wasn't aimed at him. He averted his gaze. His amped up desire was becoming a real fucking problem. The intensity of all this longing kept getting worse with every day the vacation wore on.

How could no one else on this packed island interest him?

Ducky looked down at Felicia who moved seductively close, encouraging him to dance alongside her. He did only because he saw no other choice that didn't make him come off as a giant jerk.

She was relentless in her flirting. Apparently, now making her intentions crystal clear by pushing her curvy body against his. She gave off all the right signals of being interested in whatever Ducky had in mind. He just didn't want anything from her.

"You know, if you moved to New York, you'd have a really good shot at making a modeling career for yourself," she said loudly as if the idea would tantalize him. She swayed as she turned her back to him. Her next attempt at luring him in came when she bumped her ass against Ducky.

He gave an internal eye roll that probably showed on his face.

He mimicked her move and turned his back on her, dismissing her completely. The couple behind him—now in front of him—absorbed Ducky into their circle. The song ended, and another slower beat with lots of bass began. The change in tempo slowed Ducky down too.

Like he'd done seconds ago, and like every few seconds since he'd been inside this club, his gaze landed on Chad. This time Ducky stared unabashedly. The haze in his head allowed his thoughts to wander as he mapped every inch of the guy…again.

Even in clothes that looked tailored to fit Chad's body, Ducky could see the outline of pure muscle. Of course, Chad was hot as fuck shirtless, but the clothes hinted to the allure of what was underneath and that somehow made Ducky's mouth water, his palms itching for a touch. Chad's thick bicep bulged as he lifted his glass for a drink.

Ducky looked around the table, wondering who was lucky enough to have Chad's undivided attention. Chad had a way of leaning into a person, truly listening as they spoke. Ducky had fallen into the hypnotic trap of having such a handsome face, with piercing eyes, focused only on him. Chad had a remarkable way of making a person feel special. What a unique trait for someone who only had to breathe to draw people to him.

A bump from behind brought Ducky back into his immediate surroundings. He had stopped dancing, not moving a single inch. Chad did that to him, made him lose himself in the moment. Ducky started bobbing around again as a server came by, effortlessly plucking the glass from his hand. He was forced to look away. At least for the next minute or so.

🍸

Felicia defeatedly plopped down on the empty barstool next to Chad, drawing a bark of laughter from Ava, who sat on the other side. Eric, another vacationer on the island, sat directly across from him. They had all watched when Felicia set out with purpose to finally gain Ducky's attention. As expected, she crashed and burned for the hundredth time.

Eric won the betting pool as to whether Ducky would finally take the bait. This time, Ducky had ducked out from underneath her clutches faster than any time before.

"Twenty bucks, come on." Eric stuck out his palm, wiggling his fingers, demanding his payment.

The force and outrage Felicia used when slapping Eric's outstretched hand caused a new round of laughter, all directed at her. "Shut up, Eric. You're making it worse."

Chad barely paid attention to the antics of his tablemates as he tilted the cocktail glass back, letting the ice fall into his mouth. The only person he was interested in was out on the dance floor. He crushed the small cubes between his teeth, the coldness clung to the tip of his tongue as he watched his friend on the dance floor. Ducky was a damn enigma. The guy could have anyone in this bar he wanted. Why didn't he act on any of the interest? What the fuck was going on inside Ducky's gorgeous head?

Someone's elbow hit his arm and knocked the glass away from his lips, spilling ice down the front of his shirt. He hopped off the stool to stop any potential cold wet cubes from tumbling into his lap. Which might not be such a bad thing in his current state. His traitorous dick had been giving him hell all night.

When he looked back at the table, the expectant stares halted him from lashing out. He'd clearly missed something, and no matter how quickly he'd done a rewind in his head, he couldn't figure it out. "What?"

"What," Felicia mimicked as if he were the dumbest person on the planet. Her shoulders slumped a little further forward, her back bowing as if he'd slung an insult her way. That drew a hilarious amount of laughter from Ava and Eric.

"No really, what?" Chad asked. That time he spoke to only Felicia. She seemed the only one willing to engage.

"Every girl here's been hitting on Ducky all night and all he does is stare at you." Felicia deflated again right before his eyes. If she wilted any further, she might slip underneath the table. "I've given him all my best moves. I'm everyone's type." Her hand slapped down on top of the table, driving her point home. "I'm the one who turns guys down, not the other way around."

Chad knew what a catch Ducky was, but Felicia's words confused him. As much time as he spent discreetly stalking Ducky, he'd never caught him looking back. Not once. He lifted a hand, stopping her full-on pity party before it became a full-blown narcissistic laden rant.

"What're you saying about Ducky looking at me?" Chad asked, which caused the three of them to give some sort of incredulous eye roll in unison.

Eric even burst out with a mocking laugh. A hearty sound Chad was certain had been designed to make fun of him.

"Dude, you know you can't pretend like that," Eric said. His hands flew out toward the club. "Literally everyone is talking about it tonight. Ducky's got a thing for you."

As much as his heart wanted to believe such a ridiculous notion, his head couldn't get past the obvious. "He's been out dancing with everyone tonight."

Chad's anger built with a low rumble in his core. What a cruel joke.

"Just watch Ducky," Ava intervened. "Not with that sly way you think you have. Just turn and watch him. I promise not a minute will pass before he looks at you. Try it." Challenge laced her words.

Chad didn't overthink it as he turned his gaze straight

toward Ducky. He openly stared at the bobbing head, his vision tunneled to one object of focus. An involuntary smile crept over his lips as Ducky jumped around. His friend tried to dance but that was clearly one of the few things he didn't do well.

It didn't matter. The way Ducky lit up the dance floor with his smile, using his whole body to dance regardless of the beat or style of music, held Chad mesmerized.

The evolution of that man spoke volumes. Of course, he was the hit of the club. He'd become a celebrity of sorts with the targeted advertising to this exact demographic. The old Ducky would have rejected this entire environment, certainly not put himself in the middle of the revelers.

When Ducky's gaze captured Chad's, instinct almost forced him to turn away. He stopped himself. Instead, he allowed all the feelings he'd hidden for years to show in his eyes. If Felicia and her friends were playing some sort of sick joke on him...

Ducky's face morphed through a range of emotion from confusion to uncertainty in a fraction of a second, but he didn't look away. Chad could feel the slow steady thump of his heart increase with every beat when Ducky's stare held his.

Desire ricocheted between them at lightning speed. His breath came in rapid puffs, drowning out everything standing between him and the stunning man staring back at him.

Ducky's plump lips parted.

Chad could feel the small breath Ducky took deep inside his soul.

The connection drawing him to Ducky cinched tight. Electricity crackled, the air sizzling between them. Or at least he felt it. He was so fucked over this guy.

Chad rounded the table, releasing the glass on its top, never breaking eye contact with Ducky.

As if a sea parted, Chad moved easily through the dancers. Ducky watched him closely as he barreled forward intent on his destination. Of course, the reserved Ducky hadn't moved to meet him halfway. It didn't matter. Chad would know soon enough if he'd read the signals correctly.

He reached out, curling a palm around Ducky's muscular bicep, drawing his friend forward to within inches of his chest.

Their gazes locked, possibility shining brightly. The rapid rise and fall of Ducky's chest matched his own. Chad searched Ducky's handsome face, memorizing the vulnerability reflected there. He had no doubts Ducky could see the exact look staring back at him. The years of fear of losing Ducky if he made this move melted away in an instant. His heart became the driving force in his body, demanding he win his love over.

Chad slid his free hand around Ducky's neck, keeping the hold gentle yet firm. The pad of his thumb swept the expanse of Ducky's strong jaw. The light scrape on his friend's beard sent chills racing down Chad's arm.

Oh, holy hell, the moment he'd dreamed of for more years than he could remember was finally here. Chad dipped his head forward, but he'd be damned if he rushed any part of the next few seconds.

His gaze moved from Ducky's eyes to those full, plump lips. Ducky's soft panting and the interest he'd seen flash in Ducky's eyes told Chad everything he needed to know. Ducky wanted this as much as he did, and that knowledge centered Chad, wiping any hesitation away. He slowed down, stepping into Ducky.

His lips now hovered inches from Ducky's ear. "I want to kiss you." The shiver Ducky gave seared itself into Chad's soul, urging him on. "How didn't I know until now?"

Chad grazed his cheek over Ducky's and led a caressing path back toward Ducky's mouth. His close gaze connected with Ducky's again. He saw a fire light inside those green depths. Maybe Ducky didn't appreciate the time Chad was taking to seduce him or perhaps he just wanted to move things along. Ducky's strong arm swept around Chad's waist, wrenching him closer, keeping him locked there.

Instead of taking the kiss clearly offered, Chad moved again, nuzzling Ducky's other cheek. The tender touch fueled his desire, but the way Ducky kept that arm fastened around him caused a small, satisfied smile as he breathed in Ducky's exotic scent.

The moment became complete when Ducky angled his head and sealed their lips together. The earth shifted, unbalancing him. He tightened his hold, preparing to hang on for dear life. Nothing had ever felt this right before. Instinctively, Chad swept his hands up, tracing the outline of his friend's broad shoulders until he cradled Ducky's cheeks in his palms.

Ducky opened those tantalizing lips.

Chad took the soul-searing kiss into his own hands with a vengeance. He tilted Ducky's head, driving his tongue forward into the deep recesses of that warm, inviting mouth. In one sure thrust, he claimed Ducky, laying all his intentions bare.

Stars exploded behind his closed eyelids. Fireworks shot like bullets from his brain. Damn if this wasn't better than his wildest, wettest dreams had ever dared to conjure. They were locked together in a driving exploration of each other's mouths, savoring every sizzling second.

When the velvety push of Ducky's tongue tangled with Chad's, his hips rolled forward, arching into Ducky. He was met with a long, hard cock as eager as his own. Ducky didn't shy away either. The grind of their hips had him increasing the urgency of the kiss, rutting against Chad in all the right ways.

Oh yeah! Ducky wanted him as bad as he wanted Ducky.

CHAPTER 16
SAME

Whether it be that Ducky had finally passed out from all the alcohol he'd consumed on this trip or that somehow Chad was actually standing in his arms, kissing him as if he had a right to be there, he wouldn't question his good fortune.

He centered inside himself, feet firmly planted on the ground, reveling in the most amazing moment of his entire life. Life's chaos abruptly ceased. Chad filled the missing void inside him, a place vacant for more years than he could count.

While this was not his first kiss, it was the only kiss he had ever initiated. And intuitively, he knew this one mattered the most.

Strength and purpose built within him as his arms locked around Chad, losing himself to the point he wasn't sure where Chad began and he ended.

Apparently, he was on a course to learn every dip and curve of Chad's hard body. He slid his palms from Chad's waist up the deep cords and muscles of his back. They rested on his shoulder blades, keeping Chad pressed flush against him. Chad seemed right on board with his plan.

Ducky rocked his hips back and forth, rubbing his raging hard-on against the length of Chad's rigid cock. If this was nothing more than a momentary lapse of judgment, Ducky intended to make the very most of such a gift.

The sounds around him threatened to invade this sanctuary they'd created in the middle of the dancefloor. They needed to go home. Now.

He wanted to explore the hardness in Chad's pants like he wanted to take his next breath. The thought took root, making the deep desire to taste Chad, the newest, most important goal of his life. Ducky tugged away from the kiss. Chad's hold tightened, his mouth following Ducky's until he twisted completely away.

"*Noo*," Chad moaned. His vice-like hands clamped on to Ducky's neck and jaw, urging him back into the kiss. "I've waited too long."

The simple frustrated declaration fueled Ducky's need to leave the bar as quickly as they could. To go somewhere, anywhere they could be alone. He couldn't care less where.

Why the hell had they decided to take an Uber tonight? He could have sucked the shit out of Chad from the front seat of their rental car. Frustration and longing sent a jolt of aggravation through Ducky.

"Let's go," he mouthed inches from Chad's parted lips.

Chad reared back as Ducky dragged his fingertips down his back until they grabbed both of Chad's ass cheeks. Those blue eyes turned to slate steel and Ducky was so damned mesmerized.

"Anywhere alone." Ducky was willing to go to the

darkened recesses of the parking lot mere feet away. Screw a blow job, Ducky wanted Chad in his ass, giving him everything he had, and he wanted it while looking up at Chad's handsome face.

If this was a freak moment in time, he wanted to bottom while memorizing every detail to take with him for the rest of his life.

A wicked grin spread across Chad's face. The haze of alcohol and lust made it hard to concentrate on anything more than the promise of sated satisfaction hidden within that smile.

"Not anywhere." Chad shook his head back and forth to drive the point home. "I've waited too long for this. We're doing it right. In my bed. All night long."

The tremor from such a declaration caused Ducky's cock to jerk then leak with excitement but stole his ability to speak.

"Let's go," Chad said, yet neither moved a single inch. Even with all Ducky's encouragement to leave, he was afraid if he moved, the dream would vanish into thin air.

"I don't want to let you go." Ducky whispered his confession with little hope of being heard in the din of sounds cocooning them.

Compassion and understanding crossed Chad's face. "Me either. But we gotta go if we wanna finish what we started."

Chad took the lead, turning Ducky around then nudged him between the shoulder blades, getting him moving toward the doors. Their hands intertwined, as he refused to break their connection completely. The desperation that started with the kiss added to the fever of the grip. Nothing else mattered. Not even the jeering and cheering they got on the way out. He needed this more than any other moment of his life.

♡

"Why'd we Uber tonight?" Chad grumbled, looking at his cell phone's screen for the closest ride to the bar. In his peripheral vision, he caught Ducky tucking his fingers in his pants pockets. A telltale sign that meant Ducky was drawing into himself.

Chad quickly made the selection and glanced pointedly at Ducky. Their gazes collided. He saw a thousand questions racing through Ducky's analytical head. At least that was the way he interpreted Ducky's look. For Chad, all he could focus on was Ducky's kiss-swollen lips coupled with those burning green eyes, drawing him in like a fly to honey.

He reached for one of Ducky's hands, pulling it from his pocket, threading their fingers back together. "Don't pull away."

"I wish I hadn't had so much to drink," Ducky mumbled, some serious thought trying to form on his face. "What happened in there?"

Chad guessed what Ducky actually wanted to know was what had made him finally make a move.

"I wanted that kiss for more years than you'll ever know." They were both apparently shit at reading the other's signs if near strangers had to point out an attraction that had been right before him.

Did they really need to venture into the complicated world of explanations right now?

Based on the confusion mounting on Ducky's face, he guessed the answer to his question was *yes*.

"I'm not willing to play games because I've lost too much time with you already. I'm into you. I have been for a long, long time." Chad scanned Ducky's face, his wrinkled brow. Their time in the Hawaiian sun had brought out Ducky's natural sun-kissed complexion. Chad's heart lurched in his chest, freely giving itself to the man in front of him. He stepped into Ducky's hard body until he was only inches from his beautiful face.

Ducky's eyes narrowed, as if deciphering what he'd just heard.

"I…" Ducky's hand tightened around his.

Chad lost his breath when Ducky pulled his other hand from his pocket and placed it against Chad's heart. What Ducky's words couldn't say, his actions did. The warmth of Ducky's palm against his chest burned into his soul, and those expressive eyes conveyed the exact emotion he was feeling.

"Same."

The moment he'd hoped for was going to be as sweet as he'd imagined. Chad couldn't help the grin spreading across his face. He tucked the cell phone in his back pocket so he could cover Ducky's hand still over his heart. Leaning in, he took Ducky's fleshy pout without hesitation this time. Ducky opened as soon as their lips met.

This sweet kiss spoke of the promise of what was to come before evolving into something close to X-rated. A tangle of tongue and teeth, Ducky's body pressed flush against his. What a fucking turn-on.

As Chad angled his head, the kiss consumed him. Ducky ground into him, rolling his hips. He met every thrust with one of his own. Fuck, they were going to be hot together.

A car's horn had Ducky jolting in surprise. Chad turned

toward the car and gave them an angry glare. Annoyance faded to gratitude when he saw their Uber ride had arrived.

"Back to our place," Ducky whispered huskily. He was already reaching for the back door handle of the car, giving Chad's arm a gentle tug to get him moving. Right away.

CHAPTER 17
THE SIZE

"Sorry," Ducky muttered to the driver, barely able to get the word out before Chad crawled into the backseat next to him, covering Ducky's mouth for another blistering hot kiss. The kind of kiss that made Ducky lose all sense of time and space. This time though, Chad's hands roamed freely over his body, caressing every part he could reach.

Ducky gave as good as he got, not willing to let this miraculous moment pass without learning every inch of Chad's hard body. Nowhere was off limits.

A throat clearing from the front seat drew his attention to their surroundings. Ducky tore from the kiss, taking a deep breath. He angled his head to look first at the driver who sat facing forward then out the steam-covered back window, recognizing the neighborhood of their villa. Chad's lips locked on his neck, his hand used force to bring Ducky's mouth back to his.

"We're home," he managed against Chad's insistent lips. Ducky couldn't say for sure, but that may have been the fastest ride in the history of all car rides. Thank the heavens for that. He pushed at Chad to get them both out of the passenger door.

As hard as it was to close his eyes without the world spinning, threatening his reality, Ducky managed to hang on to Chad and continue the decadent kiss as they navigated their way out of the vehicle, across the small lawn, and into the front door of their rental.

Chad had mastered the art of devastating and resolve-destroying kisses. Ducky couldn't find it in him to pull more than a hairsbreadth away. Fire built to consuming degrees, burning him from the inside out. He clutched Chad tighter, holding on in such a way to ensure this dream didn't vanish from his grasp like so many others had before.

Ducky's shirttails were yanked from his pants. Chad's strong warm hands forced their way underneath the ends of the freed material, straining the buttons in the front. The caress burned a sizzling path up his back. The skin to skin touch took this extraordinary moment to a whole new level.

Ducky's cock strained against his pants, begging him to free himself from the tight confines of his slacks and underwear. He wanted Chad's hands on him, gripping him, stroking him. Dammit if Chad wasn't some kind of mind reader, giving his greedy cock the very attention it craved.

His back struck something hard, pulling a grunt from him, but it didn't matter. Nothing mattered except this moment. Chad's palm continued the decadent touch, kneading an arousing trail up and down the length of Ducky's hard covered cock.

It felt so damn good. Too good. Addiction level good.

He dropped his chin to his chest, letting the wall at the entry of the hallway hold him upright as he watched Chad continue the skillful assault on his cock.

"Want me to free you?" Chad breathed, barely above a whisper. Certainly not said in a way of asking his permission. Chad deftly unfastened his belt and popped open the button of his pants and lowered the zipper. He yanked the binding material down past Ducky's hips.

His eager cock sprang free. Chad's hiss spoke of how much he liked what he saw, sending pleasure-filled vibrations through his body, straight up his now exposed cock.

Ducky arched his hips, his dick straining, seeking Chad's touch. His ass was bare as they stumbled their way to Chad's bedroom.

The kiss was lost when Chad cupped his cock with one hand, his head angling for the visual while the other hand pushed into the crease of his ass. He'd never felt so desired in his life.

Something close to appreciation crossed Chad's brow.

"You're huge. I'd watch you grow hard in your shorts and thought it was for someone else." Chad panted between each of his words. His hand never stopped the sensual massage. It was damned hard to stay on his feet. "Looks like neither one of us is gonna be able to walk tomorrow by the time the night's over."

The certainty of the words spoke directly to Ducky's

heart.

"I'm gonna hold you to that," he managed to say. His words were fueled by the alcohol he'd consumed, enhanced with a good dose of lust, and a lot of Chad's teasing scent causing the neurons in his head to misfire. His head swam. Chad's cologne had driven him crazy all week. "Don't worry. I give as good as I get."

Where had those words come from?

Didn't matter. He intended to make good on them.

"Promises." Chad lifted his eyes, staring at Ducky in astonishment. The heel of his palm added just the right amount of pressure to make everything right in Ducky's world. "Open my bedroom door."

Ducky lowered his hand, searching for the doorknob. He never looked away from Chad's mesmerizing gaze.

"I love your eyes," Chad confessed, further seducing Ducky with his pretty words. "When I close mine, I see yours." Chad's lust-filled gaze lifted to his hair as he spoke. "I used to dream of taking you from behind, fisting that mass of curls. My Ducky…"

Ducky slanted his mouth over Chad's as the bedroom door opened. They toppled inside. The kiss broke only long enough for Chad to pull Ducky's shirt over his head. The buttons finally gave way under the forceful tug.

Chad's chest drove him back as they both wrestled with his slacks. When the back of Ducky's legs hit the mattress, Chad gave him a shove, tumbling him down on top of the bed. The most space they'd had between them since they'd left the bar.

Chad gripped each of Ducky's shoes, flicking them off his feet and tossing them carelessly over his shoulder. His underwear and pants were then pulled down his legs. Those were tossed away too. "The problem with tight clothes, it's hard to get out of them. Scoot to the middle."

A devilishness took Chad over, his dark features turning wicked. He became the predator, chuckling a naughty, throaty sound that sent ripples of excitement through Ducky. The gleam in his eyes showed appreciation as his gaze raked the length of Ducky's body, drinking him in.

This was the exact moment he truly appreciated all the strength training he'd been doing. He wanted Chad to want him.

Ducky propped on his elbows and watched Chad peel away his clothes. His focus stayed glued to Ducky's cock. Chad hadn't had the undressing inhibitions Ducky had had during the trip. He'd seen almost all of Chad's body for days now, but the sight of Chad undressing just for him caused a full body tingle, his cock twitching and leaking under the heavy appraisal.

Chad licked his lips and said, "You're hung like a fucking horse."

The praise had Ducky gripping his cock, giving himself a long, slow pull. He wasn't sure he was worthy of such reverent praise, but he liked hearing it and seeing the way Chad watched as if he wanted him served up on a platter.

Down to only the pants covering his body, Chad took his wallet from the back pocket and dug through the folds. He produced two condoms and a packet of lube. "This is all I have. Did you bring any?"

"About the same," he murmured and nodded toward Chad's pants. "Take 'em off."

The wicked grin resurrected in full force. Chad tossed his wallet to the dresser and teased him while unfastening the hook to his pants. Those fell to the floor. The underwear followed.

Ducky's gaze locked on the jutting, cut cock angled toward him. Perfect, just like the man. Of course Chad would be flawless. Ducky dropped his head to the mattress, squeezing the shit out of his cock to stave off the urgency building there.

The mattress dipped. Ducky looked over to see Chad's knee on the bed. He began to crawl over Ducky like a wild cat, stalking and assessing his prey. He mouthed his way from Ducky's thigh to his pec. His gaze followed the trail mapped by Chad's hands and lips, touching him reverently as if he were the finest treasure on the earth.

"I want this to happen between us," Chad breathed against his pec. The tip of that talented tongue flicked across the bead of his nipple.

Ducky gave an involuntary roll of the hips.

Chad slid a hand around Ducky's neck, bringing them face-to-face. "I want you like I never wanted anything in my life."

"I can't think. It's too much to process," Ducky whispered, his panting breaths making it hard to draw in oxygen. "Please don't be a dream."

Ducky wrapped his arm around Chad's neck, locking them together. He pushed his tongue forward, easily finding Chad's for one of the most intimate kisses of his life. Truth and promise were given in a passionate clash of tongue and teeth.

Chad didn't rush or hurry, he lingered, taking his fill as

he eased down between Ducky's parted thighs, aligning his rigid length against Ducky's.

Ducky took both their cocks in his hand, stroking them together until Chad's body settled fully on top of his, caging him in. The sweet weight of Chad's body kept him from floating off the mattress in utter bliss.

Everything Chad surrounded him. Ducky was completely overwhelmed. The give and take of the kiss changed. Chad dominated, devouring him as if he'd never get enough.

Dreams did come true. His was playing out in real time.

Ducky slid his hands up Chad's back, mapping every inch of that amazing body from the small dimples at his lower back up to his strong shoulders, molding and memorizing each muscle he passed.

His effort was rewarded with a throaty moan that vibrated against his chest. Chad's tongue delved deeper inside Ducky's mouth, demanding everything he had to give.

Chad rose above Ducky, breaking free from the kiss. Ducky wasn't good at speaking his truth, but he said it all in every action and murmured protest given. They shared endless chemistry. A binding connection deeper than Chad had ever experienced before. Something told him that if they continued this course, he'd be making love today and every day that followed. He'd never get enough.

The emotion of all the unspoken words he wanted to say was almost too much to bear. He closed his eyes, drawing in deep gulps of breath, fighting the declaration of love desperate to pour from his mouth.

I've waited so long for you.

Be mine, Ducky.

I love you.

His truth.

The need to confess his devotion edged away, easier to deal with without looking Ducky in the eyes. Chad moved to Ducky's side, lying halfway on and halfway off Ducky's body. He opened his eyes to see the tip of Ducky's cock leak, little droplets forming, one right after the other under his inspection.

"I can't stop it," Ducky mumbled and reached for his cock. Chad knocked his hand away.

"You better not stop."

"Then get on with it." Ducky's legs opened wider in invitation.

Fuck yeah, Chad was back in the moment.

Ducky tangled his fingers into the strands of Chad's hair, guiding him forward. He wouldn't have necessarily called Ducky's grip a shove, but the intention was clear, he wanted Chad's mouth on his cock. Exactly where Chad wanted to be.

Chad ran his fingertips through the short, dark hairs of Ducky's groin, sending goose bumps springing up over those toned abs. He lifted, positioning himself between Ducky's thighs, mesmerized with how responsive his friend was to him.

He leaned down, licking his way across Ducky's chest, teasing each taut nipple with his tongue. His fingertips grazed up the soft skin of Ducky's thigh, leading to his sac, teasing and fondling while the other went to the base of Ducky's cock. He peppered small kisses, licks, and nips over each quivering stomach muscle on the way to his prize.

Chad lifted Ducky's cock, needing to taste his guy's essence like he needed to take his next breath. With a flick of his tongue, he swiped over the slit, taking the salty bead into his mouth.

"Oh fuck, Chad," Ducky murmured. Chad barely had a chance to open his mouth before Ducky drove his hips forward, pushing between Chad's parted lips. This time, the hand on his head didn't hold back. Chad's head was pressed forward until he took Ducky between his parted lips as deep as he could go. It was so fucking hot to be wanted this badly.

They were so in sync.

He settled back on his heels. Ducky's cock twitched as he sucked him in and out of his mouth. Chad lifted his gaze, making eye contact with Ducky who tracked every move he made.

The heat and desire reflected in Ducky's flawless face had to mirror that of his own. Chad held the intense connection. He was shit to look away.

The fear of wanting something so badly, anticipating every moment shared together, with no hope of ever truly being able to follow through, drove Chad to take Ducky deeper. Give him everything he wanted.

As much as he needed to fuck Ducky into the mattress, make his friend crave his touch, he also wanted to show the reverence this extraordinary man deserved. The inner struggle was real.

Color flooded Ducky's cheeks. His brows drew together, the hand gripping Chad's head loosened and eased down until Ducky's fingertips slid across his jaw.

"It feels too good," Ducky murmured, his voice husky and raw.

Chad bobbed his head, relaxing his jaw, moving up and down on the velvety steel length. His tongue swirled around the tip, making sure to gather every bit of pre-come into his mouth.

He released the hold he had on Ducky's balls and pushed his thumb into his warm mouth. Those perfect lips closed around the finger, sucking the digit in the same rhythm Chad sucked his cock.

Ducky was so damned responsive.

Chad took his wet thumb from Ducky's mouth to push through the crease of Ducky's ass, easily finding the tight puckered hole. He pressed there, spreading the moisture around the tight rim.

Ducky lost his mind.

"We need to now," Ducky breathed, frantically reaching for Chad.

He pulled off Ducky's cock with a pop. The intoxicated haze had vanished, leaving his love desperate. His chest heaved as a hand circled Chad's bicep.

He knew exactly what Ducky wanted and pushed his thumb past the tight ring of muscle. The world stilled as Ducky's eyes widened inches from Chad's face.

"You have to give me time. I don't want to hurt you," Chad whispered when Ducky moved his ass against Chad's thumb.

"Make it hurt good," Ducky whimpered and licked

across Chad's lips, pushing his tongue inside.

The spell was complete when Chad found the gland and pressed. Ducky's mouth dropped open, the kiss forgotten as Ducky bucked against him, tension straining his muscles.

"It feels good," Ducky growled, the back of his head hitting the mattress.

Ducky's jaw clenched before he reached for the condom, bringing the package to his lips. Ducky took matters into his own hands. Chad was shit to do more than push his thumb deeper, opening Ducky in earnest.

"I love the way you feel. I've wanted you like this for too long," Chad whispered and shifted, his cock eager for Ducky's touch. The packaging was tossed aside as Ducky lifted, taking Chad's cock in hand, deftly rolling the sheath down with expert speed.

"Fuck me," Ducky said pointedly and shifted on the bed. The intention clear, he planned to roll to his belly. No way. He wanted eye contact as he breached Ducky, made them one. Chad threw an arm out, stopping Ducky from repositioning.

"I'm looking at you when I push inside you," he demanded huskily. Ducky eyed him before lying back again, bringing his legs to his chest, exposing and opening his ass to Chad. What a beautiful sight to behold. His cock twitched, still reeling from Ducky's expert touch.

Chad forced his gaze away and reached for the lube. After generously coating his fingers, he carefully pushed two into Ducky. His gaze riveted on the hole, his lip tucked between his teeth. Tingles zipped across his skin. Ducky hadn't had a lot of action down there. He was tight and hot. So fucking hot.

He methodically worked Ducky, relaxing him open, scissoring his fingers. Ducky's swollen cock looked ready to burst, but Chad bypassed that to splay a palm across his belly. He massaged a path up to each of Ducky's nipples.

"You're gorgeous. You've always been so beautiful to me."

"You don't have to say that," Ducky said. His chest rising and falling with each panted breath.

"I know you don't believe me, but it's true. You're gonna hear it a lot," he promised, placing a hand on the back of Ducky's thighs, forcing them closer to his chest. "Don't let go."

Ducky gave a single nod, his gaze pleading for more.

"Keep your eyes on me."

"You too," Ducky hissed when Chad added a third finger. "I won't last long."

"Good thing we have plenty of time." Chad squeezed the remaining lube on his condom-covered cock, coating the length. He pressed his slick thumb past Ducky's rim, rubbing against the prostate.

"I can't..." Ducky dug his fingers into the bedspread, gripping the material, his knuckles white from the hold he had on the material. The cords and muscles in his neck and shoulders grew taut. His hips rolled into Chad. He'd waited too long. If he didn't act, this would end before they ever began.

Chad gripped Ducky's cock, squeezing tight as he positioned himself at the rim. He was met with resistance, but Ducky took matters into his own hands, bearing down on his cock, sliding his hips forward.

The effort paid off. Chad easily pushed inside with as much control as he could muster as blinding pleasure took over. Ducky took all of him with one sure thrust. White-hot heat gripped him with such intensity his eyes rolled to the back of his head.

Fireworks exploded behind the black backdrop of his eyelids. Ducky clearly knew what he was doing. The moment was too perfect. Chad's world tilted on its axis. He tried to open his eyes, to stare at Ducky as they made love for the first time, but he couldn't do it. The pleasure was too much and he damn sure didn't want it to end. Every nerve ending in his body was set ablaze. He had no idea where Ducky began and he ended.

Oh hell. How was this the most perfect moment of his life? Ducky's long arms and legs wrapped around him. The heels pushing into his ass urged him deeper. Chad was lost to do anything more than to relish this extraordinary pleasure.

"You're stretching me so good," Ducky whispered, his body moving, hips arching and rocking, gently urging Chad to participate.

All he could manage was to push his hands under Ducky's shoulder blades and grip his shoulders. The easy rhythm Ducky created now moved to the top spot of the most perfect moment of his life.

Ducky's warm breath tickled against his neck and ear. "Move with me."

Chad kept his eyes screwed tightly closed. All his concentration had to remain focused on not blowing his load before Ducky was ready to come. "I can't."

"You can," Ducky murmured, his fingers sweeping

over the bare skin on his back. "Make me come, babe."

Babe. The endearment rattled around inside his head, giving him courage to try.

Chad curled his fingers into the skin of Ducky's shoulders, anchoring his body in place as he attempted to move his hips. It took several long seconds to find the inner strength to slide out only to thrust his hips forward, back inside the delicious warm tight heat. This time his hips tucked so hard, they locked in place.

Ducky's hissed moan matched his own.

"Jeezus, Reigns…*Fuck*," Chad managed, and slowly began to roll his hips, sliding in and out of Ducky's channel.

"Yeah… Same... *Harder*."

"I don't wanna hurt you." Chad managed, his lips pressing against Ducky's collarbone. He was afraid if he looked Ducky in the eye, he'd lose the fight, come before he ever truly got started.

"You won't." Ducky shifted his hips as he answered, building speed in their thrusts.

"It feels good. So tight." Chad finally gathered enough strength to push his body back on his knees. Ducky's strong legs only let him get so far, urging his hips faster and faster.

Ducky wasn't near as silent as usual. He grunted and groaned. His eyes closed, his hands gripping Chad's forearms. Ducky was fucking himself against Chad's body, giving pleasure while taking exactly what he wanted.

Chad didn't hold back a second longer. The feel of Ducky's body quivering, fighting off his pending orgasm drove Chad to grip Ducky's cock and stroke it in time with their pistoning hips. Ducky's ass clenched around his cock, milking him, driving him deeper and harder into the tight confines.

His hand became frantic, stroking Ducky's cock with all he had to give, driving himself in and out of Ducky's hot channel. He'd never had anyone fuck him so good. Ducky bucked against him, meeting every one of Chad's thrusts until his body tensed, his hips arching against Chad. "Come with me. Chad…"

Thick creamy ribbons shot from Ducky's cock, coating Chad's hand. The smell and feel of Ducky's release and clenching ass sent Chad tumbling over the edge.

"Duncan," he moaned, falling forward. The bliss of riding out the orgasm washed all thought away. Ducky only remained, his beautiful body pulsing around his.

The entire world came to a standstill. Ducky filled in all the cracks of Chad's life. He was whole again.

As soon as he came up for air, he'd be a changed man for all the right reasons.

Ducky absorbed his body's weight. His love's arms tightened around him. His long legs tangled with Chad's.

Neither spoke for several long minutes. Breaths slowed and their heartbeats united into a single beating organ. Still, Chad remained on top of Ducky, holding him close, listening to the faint sounds of the churning ocean in the distance. He could stay this way forever.

"We're good together," Ducky murmured then gave a long, jaw-cracking yawn.

Chad agreed with both the sentiment and the yawn, wholeheartedly.

"Maybe the best of my life," Ducky added.

"Definitely the best of my life. It was perfect. Better than I ever imagined," he said, lifting his head enough to press his lips against Ducky's heated skin. "And I had imagined a lot."

"I don't bottom much." Ducky angled his head to better see Chad. His hooded gaze looked sated and exhausted.

"But you did for me."

"I wanted you," Ducky answered, lifting his arm to toss over his eyes.

"I wanted you too."

"Maybe a repeat performance?" Ducky asked, the lag in his voice suggested he was still tipsy, definitely tired. The problem was that Ducky had just given Chad the world and he wasn't tired at all.

"Ducky, I want you to hear me before you fall asleep. I want to explore this between us. When we leave here, I don't wanna let you go. I refuse to let you go. We've wasted too much time already." His hand came to Ducky's jaw, the pad of his thumb caressing against Ducky's full bottom lip. His body stirred with an unrelenting desire suggesting he might not ever get enough of this man.

"Good. Same," Ducky said. Seconds later, his body relaxed, and Ducky was out like a light.

Like the lovesick guy he'd become, Chad couldn't tear his gaze away until he was forced to roll to his side and deal with the condom. Even then, he continued to stare at the beauty finally gracing his bed.

His Ducky, who gifted him with his trust. He reached over to finger Ducky's hair, removing the small patch of unruly strands that always fell to Ducky's forehead.

"I love you," he whispered. The declaration sealed his truth, giving him the courage to finally leave Ducky's side and trust he'd be there when he returned from the bathroom. He spoke quietly as he went as if Ducky could hear him. "I needed this trip with my best friend. You've saved my life."

If only Ducky would answer with his "same" remark.

That time would come, and it would be special then too.

He had priorities. More condoms, lube, and pain reliever. The morning promised to provide competing problems for Ducky.

CHAPTER 18
THE MORNING AFTER

The tempting smell of sizzling fried bacon woke Ducky, his empty stomach rumbling in anticipation. With a deep breath, Ducky smiled on the exhale at another great trait he could add to the list of things that were fanfuckingtastic about Chad. The man could cook a good meal and seemed more than happy to do so.

He reached for his swollen lips. They were sensitive to the touch. A sweet reminder of the aftermath of their extraordinary night together.

If he'd slept more than a few hours total, he'd be shocked.

They went both ways last night. Making love, giving, and taking until the wee hours of the morning. When they slept, they stayed locked in each other's arms.

A tune by Corey Wong played low in the background. Quiet enough that he could barely hear the sounds. It had to be Corey, though. Chad played that artist's music every time he prepared food, knowing all the words and the exact moments the chords hit the sweet spot in the song.

Ducky strained to listen more closely. His smile grew wider as he made out Chad's hum or a perfectly timed grunt, whichever applied to the rhythm of the music. His heart connected, his eyes closed, and he listened to all the sounds coming from the kitchen. He bet home felt like this. What a foreign concept in his life.

He stretched, staring at his toes until his arms reached out as far as they could go. He loved the feel of all the little aches running the length of his body. Chad hadn't exaggerated. The sweet soreness in his ass spoke to the memory of Chad moving inside him over and over again.

Chad in his ass… With all the changes in his life, especially over the last few years, Chad fucking him had to be the new top insanity.

Maybe that wasn't the item in the very first spot. Chad declaring his lifelong crush on Ducky broke the ceiling of absurdity. Perhaps he was remembering parts of last night wrong. He'd heard lots of theories about sliding in and out of alternate dimensions. Maybe he'd moved into some sort of opposite parallel universe where the highly unlikely became commonplace… Seemed as likely a possibility as Chad having lifelong feelings for him.

Ducky turned, reaching for his cell phone lying half on and half off the nightstand. He lifted it to find no charge. That was all right. More than all right. He didn't want anything to mess with the peace he'd finally found inside his head. Especially not the doubt that always infiltrated from a world right outside his grasp.

He tossed the phone back on the bedside table, this time

missing the mark completely. It clanked against the tiled floor. His bad. Hopefully he hadn't cracked the screen but he couldn't find the energy to find out. The intensity of the hunger growing in his belly was what drove him from the bed.

Why hadn't he considered more sex as his cardio workouts? His stomach muscles ached as he searched the floor for his clothes, only finding a pair of Chad's athletic shorts folded at the end of the bed.

Chad's deep kisses and their frantic ways of disrobing played like an X-rated strip tease in his mind. While Ducky's head had swam with rum and the unbelievable turn of events, Chad had become a man on a mission, tossing their clothes every which way.

He'd been so lost in his own lust he couldn't quite remember the details of Chad undressing. What a loss. The guy was gorgeous both in and out of clothes. Watching him peel away each article of clothing would have been a treat all by itself. Maybe he could get a do over.

What if, for Chad, the magic hadn't held together in the daylight hours?

For all the time they had known one another, he'd been given nothing to indicate Chad was anything more than into women. They'd even shared locker room talk here and there. He didn't remember ever hearing a whisper of anything other than straight.

Doubt invaded the edges of his happy place.

Wait a minute. He hadn't discussed his sexuality with Chad either.

Chad, though, had a functioning family—not like his. Watching Dallas's daily beatings as a kid when his parents tried to wipe the gay away encouraged Ducky to always keep his lips zipped about most things. His sexual preferences first and foremost. His brother had had to sleep on the couch for years, not allowed to have his own room with the way his father watched over him for any signs of homosexuality.

Tension formed, tightening his shoulders.

Ducky blew out a forceful breath, tossing those thoughts in the recycle bin in his head where they belonged. Not a rabbit hole worth falling down.

He grabbed the shorts, quickly pushing each leg through. As he dressed, he lectured himself about the importance of going with this new flow. If they were only supposed to have last night, then he'd hold that place dear in his heart and enjoy the rest of the trip…

Just as Ducky started out of the bedroom, Chad met him in the doorway, carrying two full plates of food, silverware on the edges, and napkins tucked underneath the plates. Chad's eyes sparkled as he walked straight into Ducky, as if he had the right to be in his personal space, giving him a quick yet somehow meaningful peck on the lips.

"I tried not to wake you up. I figured you'd need some fuel after last night." Chad glanced over his shoulder toward the kitchen, a small frown furrowing his brow as he looked back at Ducky. "We should've gone to your room. It's quieter in there."

Chad side-stepped Ducky as if being together inside the bedroom was the most natural thing in the world and made his way to the bed. One plate was placed on top of the bedside table on the opposite side Ducky before Chad turned back to him.

His bright eyes were crystal clear with assuredness until he looked back at Ducky then paused. The dark brows furrowed again, assessing him more closely, giving a full body scan from head to toe, only stopping briefly in the region of his plumping cock. The shorts did little to hide his erection.

Clearly, a single night of dreams coming true wasn't enough to sate his desire for his best friend.

Oh, fuck! What were they going to tell everybody? None of their friends were going to believe this one.

"You're overthinking," Chad stated as only someone who knew him well could do.

"It's a lot," Ducky replied in complete contradiction to his mental commitment moments ago to just go with the flow.

But what did the flow actually mean? Who flowed with anything? Dallas flowed with the terms his parents put on him as an adolescent, but he bided his time to get out of the house and never looked back… The flow sucked. Who would want to flow around?

The concern on Chad's face grew more pronounced as he placed the second plate on the edge of the mattress and walked slowly back to Ducky as if he were some sort of skittish colt ready to bolt.

That alone was the comic relief he needed. He shook his head, dispelling the frantic emotions that took over as he bypassed Chad and went for the food. "I'm trying not to overthink but it's hard. Are you going with it?"

"I'm more than going with it. I meant everything I said last night," Chad said, trailing behind. His tone had no hesitation, only clear and determined.

Okay. What did that mean?

Ducky sat on the edge of the mattress, lifting his gaze to Chad who stood before him, just out of reach. All that handsomeness messed with his head too. On instinct alone, he mimicked Chad's earlier perusal as he looked up and down his friend's body. A mouthwateringly hard body.

Want and desire edged out the doubt. Flashes of memory of Chad moving over him, whispering words of love in his ear, the devotion implied in their love making… "We'll have to hit the highlights of last night. I might have missed a few things." Ducky pushed the plate out of the way.

Chad broke the invisible line between them, taking the step forward, nudging his legs apart to stand in the middle of his thighs. Calm returned. His mind stilled. He boldly reached for Chad's hips, drawing him closer. This time, he gave a pointed stare at Chad's cock, the hard-on tenting the thin material of his shorts.

"Want me to take care of this?"

"More than anything else in the world." Chad's hands came to rest on Ducky's shoulders, letting him take the lead.

He pushed the elastic waistband of the shorts down Chad's legs. With the tips of his fingers, he followed the perfect curve of Chad's ass until he reached the short hairs on the back of Chad's thighs. He skimmed his fingers across the warm skin, watching with fascination at the efforts of his foreplay.

Chad's plumping cock zinged to hard as hell in seconds flat.

With a groan, Chad's hand rose to Ducky's neck. The pad of his thumb lovingly swept across the edge of his hairline, eliciting goose bumps down his back. Chad's other hand grazed over his jaw, lips, and cheekbones, reverently.

Ducky cradled Chad's sac, adding pressure while he curled his other hand around the jutting cock. A tiny bead of pre-come gathered at the top, thrilling him. Somehow Chad did in fact want him. This moment exemplified that, even more so than any words they could have spoken. Ducky swallowed the lump of excited anticipation swelling in his throat and parted his lips. With a flick of his tongue, he lapped away the salty evidence of Chad's need then watched as another droplet formed at the slit. Ducky licked that drop away too.

"If you put me in your mouth, I'll tell you what I said last night," Chad bartered. His tone was flirtatious and husky and full of desire.

"Not necessary. I'm remembering now." Ducky meant those words. He had seven days left on this trip. If, when they left, this part of their relationship was left here too, then Ducky wanted every single moment of their time together to be embedded in his mind.

Oh fuck. As hard as Chad tried to watch his dick disappearing inside Ducky's skilled mouth, he was shit to do more than tighten his grip on Ducky's head to help keep himself upright. His eyes rolled into the back of his head. Pleasure swept from his cock to all parts of his body. Talk about toe-curling…

They'd had each other many times last night, but he could surely last a few minutes without having to fight back his release. Clearly, that was a laughable thought. Before he had any chance to pull himself together, Ducky's velvet tongue curled around his tip then plunged his cock deep inside his mouth. His balls tightened, his fingertips dug into the soft skin of Ducky's neck, and he hissed out a grunted breath. *Jeezus.*

The next pull had Chad hitting the back of Ducky's throat. Who would have thought Ducky lacked a gag reflex? The man was full of surprises, delightful surprises.

Focus, Chad demanded of himself. He clamped his jaw shut, ground his teeth together, and locked his eyelids closed. His senses sizzled, coasting close to overload. He didn't stand a chance to last as long as he wanted if he continued to watch Ducky bob his head. He drove Chad's cock in and out of his mouth.

Ducky's grip tightened at the base of his cock, guiding the blow job with skill. That tongue, made for pure pleasure, circled Chad's tip, adding to the slick ride back into the warm confines of Ducky's mouth. The hand at his balls knew exactly what he wanted, a soft gentle touch with a good, tight tug thrown in for good measure. Chad wanted their love making to always have this sense of urgency, where neither seemed able to get enough or hold back on the other.

His fingers loosened their hold, cupping Ducky's jaw. He swept the pad of his thumbs under the soft skin of Ducky's eyes and cheeks. Ducky added a hard squeeze to his sac. Chad was shit to stop his cock from leaking as a kaleidoscope of fireworks burst from behind his eyelids.

Chad panted, his fingers digging into Ducky's neck, jaw, and stubbled cheek. Images of his dreams from the past fueled his desire. Ducky's longer curly hair sliding between his fingers played in his mind's eye like the fantasies he'd always had of this man. He followed the trail of short hairs up to the longer-on-top silky strands. He clutched the tresses, fighting the need begging him to take control.

"Grow your hair out for me," Chad groaned. The words cost him some of his restraint. He clamped his jaw closed, dropping his chin to his chest. As much as he wanted to demand Ducky's immediate agreement, to have this man promise to be with him until the short strands were long and full again, he was shit to do anything more than ride the pleasure.

"Tug," he whispered, cracking his eyes open. Ducky's head rolled back and forth. Those plump lips that looked made for sin were exactly as Chad had imagined. His hips began a barely controlled thrust, pushing deeper into Ducky's mouth. It was time to put an end to this tantalizing agony. "I want to lose myself…" He couldn't finish because holy fucking hell if Ducky didn't loosen his jaw, opening his throat. His hips bucked as Ducky swallowed around him, his throat twitching around Chad's cock.

"I want you, Duck…" Chad's head swam, making it hard to send words out into the world past the jumble of sensations running through his body. "This is right. You and me. Together."

Desire surged through Chad as swift as the fire racing through his veins. Ducky moaned. The vibration slid down his cock, showing him how much Ducky liked what he said. He'd never had sex where it felt so damn right that he wanted this exact moment repeated again. A lifetime of getting off with his best friend. The person who mattered most…

All thought dissolved as primal instinct took over. He fucked Ducky's mouth like he'd taken his ass last night.

"Move back," he growled.

Ducky lifted his gaze, a single eyebrow arched in challenge. He started to pull off Chad while lifting his ass off the mattress. That was the exact opposite of what he wanted. Chad locked a hand on the back of Ducky's neck and head, keeping him covering Chad's cock as he placed a knee on the mattress. His hips kept the pace as he crawled onto the bed, pushing Ducky to his back until he straddled his face.

The clanking of the breakfast plate landing on the floor registered somewhere in the back of Chad's mind. Fuck the food. Who needed to eat? If this was all he did for the rest of his life, he'd die a happy man. For good measure, he gave in to the controlled thrust of the hips, letting the desire dictate his motions, driving deeper down Ducky's throat.

"You good?"

Of course, Ducky couldn't speak but he lifted his palms to the back of Chad's thighs, caressing until his hands clasped the globes of Chad's ass and squeezed his approval.

Chad fell to his hands, his hooded gaze kept watch on his dick as he fucked in and out of Ducky's mouth over and over again. How did this feel like the best moment of his life?

Ducky. Duncan. Both names rattled around his brain, driving up the pleasure of his pending orgasm. Ducky pressed a finger against his rim, breaching him there. The tip easily found and massaged his gland.

Chad lost it. Darkness haloed his vision. His head swam in the decadence as sensation assaulted him from all directions. The orgasm he'd battled burst free, surging forward, incapacitating him with blinding speed. He was unable to do anything more than lift his hips to pull from Ducky's mouth.

Ducky's grip on his ass turned vise-like. Ducky locked on to him, keeping him inside that talented mouth. The release now sweeter as he poured himself down Ducky's throat.

For the briefest of seconds, Ducky's throat contracted around Chad. Time slowed. He could feel every pulse of his release. Ducky's thundering heartbeat matched his own. His senses were alive, completely aware of every breath and movement Ducky made. His lover's fingers skimmed down the short hairs of Chad's thighs, causing them to stand on end. Ducky's mouth loosened its hold on Chad's cock, his breath panting into Chad's groin, sending chills zinging all over his sensitive body.

A sated haze took over, causing Chad to push himself over until he landed with a thud on his back, his hand reaching for any part of Ducky he could touch. His eyes were screwed tightly shut. He had no idea how much time passed as he lay there basking in the wonderment of the moment.

Only when his hand fell to the mattress and Ducky

pushed forward, climbing out of bed, did Chad try to tune in enough to crack his eyelids and lift his head marginally.

"Come back." The weight of lifting his head was too much to manage and dropped backward, cushioned into the soft mattress. He kept his gaze on Ducky when he patted the bed next to him, hoping to give incentive. "I owe you one. Give me a minute…"

Ducky gave a husky chuckle, carefully removing his underwear off his body. "I got off. I couldn't help myself." His fascinating friend lifted the folded underwear up his body, swiping his belly as if to drive the point home. Chad closed his weary eyes. Wonderment turned to sheer luck. He managed to get Ducky off without touching him. As soon as he woke from the fifteen-minute cat nap he planned to take, he'd tell Ducky exactly how fire he thought that was.

CHAPTER 19
ENTER WILDER

Chad sat side by side with Ducky at the patio table, so close he was able to lift Ducky's hand, keeping it close as he finger-played with each of Ducky's digits. In all the days they'd been on vacation together, this hour, late in the afternoon, had become Ducky's meditation time. He usually sat quietly on the beach by himself, staring out at the ocean, seemingly lost to the thoughts inside his head.

He had no idea why Ducky hadn't gravitated toward his usual spot this afternoon, instead choosing to stay cuddled up next to him. Maybe he had come off as too needy. Only wanting to be glued to Ducky's side until enough time passed where they could meander their way back toward the bedroom and stay there the rest of the night.

He had only thought he had it bad for Ducky. After last night, and then again this morning... Well, he found reason and purpose within him. The exact combination of clarity as if Ducky was somehow his missing link to everything. He narrowed his eyes under the heavy implication of what a thought like that meant for his future.

As ready as he was for this kind of relationship with this particular man, he feared coming on too strong and pushing Ducky away. His fingers tightened around Ducky's, committing the promise to his heart that he'd do whatever it took to keep Ducky happy and by his side. Even if they were nothing more than friends with benefits.

The violent lurch of his heart dragged his lips down into a frown. He lifted Ducky's hand to his mouth, kissing the warm skin of his fingers. In his peripheral vision. He caught Ducky's gaze leaving the ocean to turn a questioning glance his way. He had to look at Ducky, seeing the piercing gaze that spoke of love, determination, and commitment to his heart which seemed a fickle fucking organ with the way it flipped emotion around today. The tension from seconds ago eased under the weight of Ducky's concerned stare. All he could do was give the smile Ducky responded to the most.

"I like this between us. I don't want it to end after we leave here."

Ducky's expression turned quizzical, making Chad wonder if he was the only one thinking long term. Perhaps he was—something he tended to do a lot—jumping way ahead, analyzing all the angles and possibilities.

"I've made some decisions about my life that I don't think are going to go over well," Ducky said, pulling his hand from Chad's. He found it hard to tamp down the urge to hold on tighter. He watched as Ducky crossed his arms over his chest. Ducky seemed to get smaller in front of him. Whatever decisions were made had Ducky unsure.

The need to offer comfort pushed him. Chad reached over, cupping Ducky's thigh with his palm, he squeezed. He scanned Ducky's tanned face which was paling by the second. "I can't imagine anything that you do will disappoint me."

A single harsh laugh forced itself from Ducky's lips, but Chad's words did seem to help the tension that had suddenly formed between them. Ducky's shoulders loosened until they slumped, his gaze shifting back to the ocean, letting Chad know he had only changed his location of meditation, not the actual act of meditating.

"I'm not into the life I'm living," Ducky stated strongly then hedged in saying anything more. He opened his mouth as if to say more then closed it.

Chad caressed his palm back and forth over Ducky's thigh as he tried in vain to manage the tightness overtaking his heart. Reasonably, he understood that he needed clarification of Ducky's words before he let his own emotions spiral, adding negative meaning to Ducky's simple declaration.

"I liked myself better before I started making all this money," Ducky finally said.

Chad only nodded, not really connecting the dots between now and then. From Chad's perspective, Ducky had changed very little about his life even with all his successes. His world literally revolved around the same five miles he'd grown up in. The tight grip on his heart eased as he agreed with the parts he understood. "I liked you before too, but I don't think you're that different of a person."

Ducky unwound his hands from the hold he had around his chest, placing a palm on his heart. "I'm different here, and I don't like it." Ducky's angry brow furrowed, the look on his face hardened as he got to his feet, moving completely away from Chad. He took long strides to the railing of the patio, giving Chad his back as he stared out at the ocean for several long minutes.

With the same anguished flare, he turned back toward Chad, leaning his ass on the ledge. His arms crossed over his chest again. He looked ready for an argument. "I'm giving my money away. I don't like it. People suffer while I have all this cash that I don't need. I'll increase our company's benefit packages then I'm giving the rest to charity. Greer knows lots of nonprofits who are trustworthy…" Ducky shook his head as his lips clamped shut. His strong jaw ground together. The direct focus Ducky had on Chad let him know this decision somehow included him.

"I only need about twenty thousand dollars a year to live on. I don't like the excess or the way it causes people to look at me differently now. I want to live an authentic life, one that represents me, not everyone else."

Chad could do little more than nod as he got to his feet. Of course, Ducky wouldn't like having money. He'd always railed against the world for not taking care of the underprivileged. He hadn't ever met anyone in his life who considered everyone before themselves, but Ducky did. He inspired Chad to look at the world differently, always do better in his day-to-day life.

Before he said those exact words, he needed to better

understand his involvement in Ducky's changes. As much as he hated to, Chad stopped short again of reaching for Ducky. This time, fisting his hands to force them to stay by his side.

"Do you think I see you differently?" Chad asked.

"Do you?" Ducky shot immediately back. "Are you sure that's not driving this between us?" Whatever look Chad gave had Ducky lifting a hand between them in some sort of peace offering wave. At least his voice lost the accusatory tone as he finished his explanation. "Not intentionally. I know you're not that kind of person but consider the possibility. I don't have any real friends anymore. People look at me differently. I never expected to be making this kind of money in my life."

"Fuck no, I'm not seeing dollar signs when I look at you."

Ducky had never seen himself clearly. His lack of confidence in himself, and in Chad for that matter, made him step forward, his chest touching Ducky's crossed arms.

"I don't want your money. I want you." His hands reached out of their own accord, gripping Ducky's biceps. It just felt better to be touching him. "You're my best friend. I went nuts when you weren't talking to me. I've stayed away from you all these years because it's really real for me. These days of this vacation have been the best but hardest of my life. You're fucking perfect, Duck…"

Ducky unwound his arms, both palms came to his chest. Close to his heart, effectively stopping him from saying anything more. "You have to see we make no sense."

"What doesn't make sense?" Chad shot back, shaking his head, giving an exaggerated eye roll to make sure Ducky got the absurdity of such a statement. "What you *just said* doesn't make sense. You've never seen yourself clearly."

Chad's anger sparked, fueling more of his truth to tumble from his lips.

"Give your money away. Take care of the world. You're the only one of us who's surprised at your decision. I damn sure make more than twenty thousand dollars a year, and I'm about to make a whole lot more with WS. I got you. I can support us." He took a small step forward, bumping against Ducky's chest. The frantic beat of Ducky's heart matched the thundering one in his own chest. Lust and love were no longer the only things motivating Chad. He was frustrated yet never more certain of anything in his life.

He had to take a second to rewind his words to find which ones may have caused Ducky's current look of alarm.

"You just said your life's changed. You're alone all the time. Give up your apartment and move in with me." Chad refused to accept Ducky's stunned expression as anything more than surprise. They made sense, regardless of what Ducky had conjured up in his head. "I have a second bedroom if that helps ease whatever caused that look on your face."

Chad wrapped his arms around Ducky's waist like a vise, keeping them pressed together even as his tone changed to reflect the sincerity of his idea. "You aren't the only one with head issues about the course of your life.

I've been tilted too, but you've helped settle me. I know what I want. My vision is clear. You just need to catch up."

Ducky's troubled stare locked on Chad. His lips parted, letting out a puff of warm breath that hit Chad square in the face. "What do you want?"

He couldn't help this second crazy eye roll he gave. How did he say a lifetime without sending this sweet, nonsensical man running?

Chad decided to let action give his answer. He leaned in, taking Ducky's lips in one of their uniquely heated kisses. There was no hesitation on Ducky's part. He opened for Chad, wrapping his arms around him too, accepting everything offered. No matter what they said, this kiss proved they were on the exact same page.

Love and promises exchanged between them with the touch of lips.

Ducky tightened his arms around Chad, hanging on to him.

He leaned forward, pushing Ducky back against the rail. His body grew tense with need, wanting to give this commitment then seal their fate in the bedroom.

No wonder he was the ideas guy. That was clearly the best idea ever.

Maybe the only thing that might tear Chad from this soul-destroying kiss would be getting them back to the bedroom. He pulled away, lifting a hand to Ducky's jaw to keep him from following. Ducky's lust-filled gaze searched Chad's face until they stared one another in the eye. He needed Ducky looking at him before reason lost to the desire ricocheting through every nerve ending in his body.

"I know I love you. Give all your money away. Do what's best for you. I'll respect the decisions you make. All I ask is that you keep me in your life. It's the only place I want to be."

Tension melted off Ducky. He relaxed against the railing, his face going through a range of emotion before settling on something close to resolve.

"Same." The simple declaration made Chad smile even knowing he'd have to hear more from Ducky later, his heart required it.

Chad sealed their love with a press of the lips. Then another and another. Ducky's palms cradled Chad's face, keeping him close as they kissed again, this time longer, lingering, and filled with the passion that seemed to accompany every single kiss they shared.

"You made it easier," Ducky murmured when Chad broke away to take a breath. "Thank you."

"The pleasure is mine. I finally got what I wanted," Chad said. "We're in this together now."

Ducky took him into a hug. The only outside world interference that could have penetrated this moment was the loud, shrill ringtone Chad had assigned his sister, Chloe. A binging buzz that grated over every one of his nerves just the way her voice did. Ducky looked away, toward the villa, trying to place what made such an annoying clatter.

"Ignore it. It's Chloe." The ring ended only to begin again.

"What's that awful noise?" Both he and Ducky jerked their heads around to see Felicia and Ava trudging through the sand, close to the villa.

He'd meant to cancel their gathering tonight. Ducky stood to his full height but seemed as reluctant to end their embrace as Chad.

When the ringtone ended only to begin again for the third time, Chad finally let go of Ducky, turning toward the villa. "Goddammit. I'll be right back."

"Hey," Felicia said. Ava mimicked her friend in a much more sedate voice. Ducky didn't turn away from watching Chad's retreating body until he disappeared through the doorway and could no longer be seen. The haze of their confessed love drowned away everything else around him. His eyes searched the open door, hoping Chad would reappear as the lifesaver he clung to.

Chad loved him. Tingles raced head to toe over his body as his chin hit his chest. He reveled in all the special feels, his body giving a full-length shiver even under the warmth of the day. Nothing had ever felt so right in his life. A true balance settled over him. Something new and complete, satisfying and cherished.

In the back of his mind, the dark place created by years of being told he wasn't good enough by his father and oldest brother made him question everything. With all the self-lecturing he'd done for the length of this trip, feeling inadequate in every way to Chad, he couldn't let it go until right this very minute. He wondered if Dallas had these same feelings when he settled down and accepted Greer as his partner?

What a fucking turn-on to be wanted as you were.

"He's mad at us," Felicia said loud enough to infiltrate Ducky's focus. "It's not fair, Ducky. I didn't know you were into guys."

"It makes sense though." The way Ava said the words caused Ducky to look over at her. Her hands, one holding a cell phone, lifted in a surrender as if she had offended him. "Everyone kept hitting on you and you never bit. That's all I'm saying, I promise. We're all sad you're gay."

"Yeah. We didn't know." Felicia stepped closer to the railing next to Ducky. "Apparently no one knew. You're good at hiding. You should've put us out of our misery."

Ava playfully slapped at his arm, coming to stand on his other side. "Why didn't you tell us Chad's dad owns Wilder. I feel like that was something we needed to know."

"I'm not in the gamer world but how didn't I remember Chad as the guy who dragged you hard after that award show?" Felicia added.

Ducky's eyes narrowed. His entire focus tuned into Ava's words. His head swiveled in her direction. He was having a hard time thinking beyond Chad but couldn't remember anything said to tip Chad's hand. "How do you know that?"

Shit. His question was barely out when dread filled the deepest recesses of his mind. That said a lot, Chad had embedded himself in all of Ducky's thoughts.

"My video's been viewed and shared two hundred forty thousand times on Secret. It's gone everywhere," Felicia answered cryptically with a sheepish grin.

Fuck! It all made sense.

Chad came through the back door, his troubled stare riveted on Ducky though he held his phone raised in his hand. Chloe's voice spoke about a mile a minute on a video call. He'd heard both Chad's sisters talking in the background many times over the years. Chloe had never sounded so frantic before. "Mom and Dad have both been trying to get a hold of you. The video's the number one post on Secret since it posted last night. Everybody knows who Ducky is because of the ad campaign. It took about an hour for the users to figure out that Ducky was kissing you. That drew Wilder into the mix too. It exploded from there."

"It's the number one video on Secret?" Felicia gasped excitedly. All the sorrow she pretended to have vanished into thin air. She gave a happy little giggle before bringing her phone forward, working her thumbs furiously over the screen. "I put it on TikTok too."

"Is it a real kiss, Chad?" Chloe asked. Ducky couldn't tell by her tone what she thought of the idea. Chad came to stand directly in front of Ducky, lowering the phone between them where he could see Chloe as the primary caller, but Cate was bent over Chloe's shoulder. Cate and Chad had always been the two closer siblings.

"Chad, you don't have to answer that," Cate called out, bending closer to the screen, reaching for Chloe's phone. "Is that Ducky with you?"

"What?" Chloe shrieked, moving the phone out of Cate's reach. Neither of the sisters were now on screen. "He does too have to answer that. I wanna know." He couldn't see much except there seemed to be a struggle for the phone. These two accomplished young women were now in a row for the cell phone, reverting to that unique place where siblings fought regardless of the situation.

"No matter what you think, Chad's allowed to have his privacy," Cate reprimanded.

"Our brother's possibly bisexual. It's kind of important to know," Chloe countered as if Cate was the dumbest person on the planet.

"It's none of your business," Cate said. This time, when she reached for the phone, she managed to pluck it from Chloe's hand.

Cate darted away, the phone capturing video of the walls, floor, and ceiling before a door slammed, plunging the video into darkness. Chloe's outrage became muted at the same time as a light came on and Cate's face reappeared on the screen.

"I'm sorry about her. I tried to call you several times since last night to warn you. The video went viral on Secret and on StreamTrainer's platform. You were live streamed with you two kissing pretty hot and heavy then leaving together. Dad didn't see the post until this morning. Somehow Mom and Tristan both knew about you and Ducky before Dad. I think his feelings were hurt."

As self-focused as Ducky became on this trip, all that faded away as Chad's usual smile morphed into a deep-set frown. He stayed quiet, waiting for Chad's reaction. Ava tugged at Felicia's arm, pulling her off the porch, seeming to understand the privacy they needed.

"I only told Mom a few days before we came to Hawaii." Chad lifted his sad expression to Ducky. "I talked to her about it when you weren't talking to me.

She's the one who urged me to come see you at your office that night."

"I wasn't purposefully not talking to you," Ducky said, wanting to provide some sort of comfort, but Chad cut him off.

"I know, but I didn't tell you that I told her I was into you. That's how she knows."

"How does Tristan know and not Dad?" Cate asked. A really good question. "You don't have to answer. Call Dad. He's in protection mode. He's broken his rule on allowing free speech to dictate the news feed on Secret. He's tried to suppress the video until he could talk to you but the buzz around Ducky's ad campaign and the way StreamTrainer is going nuts over it all means Dad hasn't been successful. I guess Ducky's the one in StreamTrainer to make the decision to mute the post. His brother's been trying to call him too."

Well shit. Ducky pushed off the railing, going in search of his phone. The complete technology reprieve of the last twenty or so hours now felt more like a nightmare than the peace it had offered at the time. He went to his bedroom, pushing open the door only to remember he hadn't been in there since he left last night for the bar. He pivoted around, bumping against Chad's chest.

"Do you know where my phone is?"

"I'm sorry," Chad said by way of an answer.

"What're you sorry for?" Ducky asked, bypassing Chad. Maybe three steps into the living room, the fairytale of minutes ago took a hard, plunging nosedive. "Did you want us to keep this a secret?"

Emotionally, he hadn't gotten too far into what a

relationship with Chad might mean, but he didn't see himself as willing to be a side piece or a hidden secret.

"No," Chad said firmly, trailing after him. "I just have daddy issues."

Ducky let those words bounce around his head before he stopped in the doorway of Chad's bedroom. Only then did he remember he'd dropped his phone to the floor on the other side of the bed. It had no charge. But that took second place to the reality of Chad's response. He swiveled around, walking backward to the nightstand, saying, "Your dad's crazy about you. He only helped us with StreamTrainer because of you."

Chad nodded as if that explained it all. He followed Ducky, moving within inches of his body, making it hard to concentrate. The personal space between them no longer seemed to matter. An arm hooked around Ducky, halting his progress. "I didn't say it was justified. I don't like to think about it. It makes me feel ungrateful. I'm not exaggerating at all when I say I was into you when we were young. I had to reconcile all these feelings about my sexuality all by myself. Then Dad came out and there came the media circus, lost friendships, and my family breaking apart. I've been with other men but kept my secret from my parents. It's hard to leave that mindset."

Yup, he got that perfectly. It was damn hard to let go of the past, but if they didn't try, how could the future be anything other than a continuation of the chaos all around them?

His identity as a person required him to live a genuine, honest, and truthful life. No longer trying to make everyone around him happy at the expense of himself.

Chad had to be on the same page if they had any real chance of making it work between them. A sense of strength built rapid-fire within him.

"Then we have to deal with it in order to move forward." He ducked away from Chad, going for his phone. "After you deal with your dad, then explain to me how you justified learning you were into guys because of your feelings for me, yet you decided to bang other guys that weren't me…"

The tension that had formed around them dissolved as Chad barked out a laugh. "I thought you were straight. I saw it as unrequited love. Don't be getting any ideas for the future. We're monogamous."

What Ducky hadn't expected as he picked up his phone off the floor was the sound of bare feet running toward him. Chad executed a perfect tackle, taking him off his feet, causing him to land hard on the top of the mattress. He bounced into Chad's solid body as it came down on top of his.

He'd been tackled more times than he could count as a rite of passage earned by being the youngest of three brothers, but this one he let happen without fighting back. Chad manhandled him until he lay on his back, arms pinned above his head and Chad straddling his belly, looming above him. It might have been the most beautiful sight of his life. "Say we're monogamous."

"We're in an open relationship," Ducky quipped back, biting his lip to hide his grin. The silly joke tasted like acid on his tongue.

"I'm gonna kiss that smirk off your face," Chad threatened as if that were a real punishment.

"My ass is smirking too," Ducky teased challengingly. With an arch of Chad's brow, he lowered his head, lips hovering just above his.

"So we'll deal with life later?" Chad countered, letting go of one of Ducky's hands. He rose enough to push his hand between his thighs, slipping underneath the waistband of his shorts.

His hard-on turned to steel. Who cared about the video or the world trying to trespass into their paradise? Ducky rolled his hips when Chad's fingertips touched the head of his cock.

"Rim me and you got a deal."

"You know the language of love, don't you?" Chad lifted to push down Ducky's athletic shorts. Those were tossed toward the only chair in the room.

Chad fisted Ducky's cock, his mouth lowered, slanting over Ducky's.

Better if all life just handled itself and left them alone.

CHAPTER 20
CLOTHING OPTIONAL

"Tristan kept my secret," Chad called from the bathroom off his bedroom. Ducky lay in the bed, still coasting on his release. He'd never had this much sex in this short of time in his life. Chad was a tank in the bedroom. His boundless energy drove their pleasure to crazy heights.

How could the guy even stand after the power bottom performance he'd just given? Chad had taken all Ducky had to give. How was that even possible? His eyelids slid closed. He was so blissed out he didn't bother to try to stay awake.

"You know, it was your fault. If I'd had some warning… Are you asleep?"

Ducky kept his eyes closed but tucked his lip between his teeth, trying to manage the size of his smile as he kicked the bedspread up with his foot, covering the bottom half of his body. The action seemed to be reply enough.

"No way." Chad caught the blanket before it fully encased him in its downy comfort. "We're dealing with family then going for a jog on the beach."

Ducky's brow furrowed, the smile gone in a flash, trying to remember if he'd promised to go running at any point. Jogging was his least favorite physical activity. He'd rather play *Call of Duty* in a tournament with a toddler before he ran anywhere. One eye cracked open to see Chad plugging a charger into his cell phone.

"I don't wanna run. I feel like I enjoy watching you run better. Everybody likes to watch you run. That's why we keep having all those parties at the house. You draw them to us."

"Are you flirting with me? Trying to distract me?" Chad asked teasingly.

"Is it working?" He guessed not as his cold, hard cell phone landed on his belly.

"I achieved the feat of having my sexy best friend fall for me. I'm ready to tell the world. You and I jogging on the beach says it all." Chad leaned down to kiss Ducky with a smack on the lips. His retreating footsteps had Ducky finding the energy to open his eyes and lift his head to watch Chad's naked ass bounce as he left the bedroom.

What a perfect ass...

The guy didn't have an ounce of fat on him. Probably due to all the jogging.

Interesting. Not the incentive Ducky thought it might be to get him to do any kind of running. He dropped his head back on the pillow, stating the obvious, loud enough to be heard. "Apparently the world already knows."

Chad came strolling back inside the room, downing a

water bottle. He tossed a cold bottle toward Ducky. His aim was perfect, landing with a thump then a roll on his chest. The chilled bottle against his heated skin instantly made him jerk upright, one hand grabbing his phone to keep it from falling. The other reached for the near frozen water bottle as it slid down his side, leaving a cold, wet trail as it went.

"What the hell, Reeves?"

His answer came by way of a chuckle. Chad pulled a T-shirt from the closet. Another was tossed toward Ducky. "You should probably run your fingers through your hair. I'm not FaceTiming my dad alone. He likes you, probably better than me."

Chad's determination to deal with their problems finally made Ducky leave the bed. One of the things this vacation had taught him was that life away from the monitor was way more peaceful than what went on behind the screen.

"When my family broke apart over Dallas coming out gay, I was pretty torn up. Donny was acting a fool, posting all this crap about Dallas and StreamTrainer on social media. Your dad called to check on me and let me vent. His advice was to stay off social media until it blew over. He kept insisting social media wasn't real. Its development was designed to connect friends and family together, but the extremist took over, making it into something no one really wants. He helped me. Your dad's a good man. I wish he was my father."

Ducky pulled the T-shirt over his head, thinking about how much Dylan Reeves, and Tristan Wilder for that matter, had guided him, giving him courage to continue.

Outside of his brother, Dallas, those two men were probably the only people in the world to believe in him. Well now he knew Chad did too.

"Quit stalling." A baseball cap flew like a frisbee through the air, hitting him in the chest.

"Sorry. I was just thinking…" he didn't finish his sentence because when he looked over at Chad, he lost his train of thought.

Chad was fully dressed now. Pulling off relaxed casual in a T-shirt and pressed shorts, but like normal, he looked like he'd walked off the cover of some preppy fashion magazine.

"Do I get a pair of athletic shorts?" he asked, tossing out his hands to showcase his exposed penis. "Probably not the best look for talking to your dad."

"I don't know. I like you like that. We'll be careful with the screen," Chad said as if that were a real option. His eyes remained fixed on Ducky as his voice deepened to almost a growl. Ducky's traitorous cock plumped under the appraisal. "How were you so good at hiding that thing? You're huge."

Chad's appreciative smile grew and so did Ducky's.

With all this grinning, if he didn't do something, they'd be right back in bed. The way Chad liked to worship his ass, he wouldn't be able to walk properly for a good week. Tempting, but… Oh hell, he rolled his eyes at all his recent self-reflection. They had to adult at least for the next couple of hours.

He grabbed the ball cap with a huff, and side-stepped Chad as he extended his hand in invitation. His intentions were clear. They could put the calls off again. "No. Calls first.”

“Hey, you didn’t even want to make the calls in the first place,” Chad countered, watching Ducky leave the room. He didn’t follow which meant he saw merit in Ducky’s words.

“Meet me in the living room. I’m not doing this in your bedroom.”

How long would it take to be able to look at Ducky and not want him so badly it physically hurt? Never seemed the best answer. Especially now that he knew how fluid they were together both in and out of the bedroom.

But Ducky wasn’t wrong. To keep the stress at bay, to continue this honeymoon phase of their lives, they needed to make these phone calls. After that, they had another seven days to keep the outside world at a distance. At least, he hoped with all his heart that it worked that way.

Chad had to ball his fists together to keep from running his fingers through his freshly styled hair under the worry and anxiety they possibly faced. Ducky hadn’t had an easy life and deserved better. More than anything else, he wanted to be a source of peace for Ducky.

Determination made him pick up his cell phone, ignoring the silent rapid-fire notifications crossing the screen as he searched his recent calls. He had nine missed calls from his father. The same amount from his mother. Tristan had only sent one text message.

Chad opened the text first. Four simple words that built confidence in his decision. *“I’m proud of you.”*

Tears filled his eyes. His family's unconventional life had had the potential to implode around them. Instead, the commitment they all had for one another built a super-functional blended family. Tristan couldn't be a better parental figure. Chad quickly typed his true appreciation, *"I needed to hear that, thank you. I'm calling Dad now. Is it a good time?"*

The man who owned the world, operated multiple large businesses with an employee base of several hundred thousand people worldwide, always put his family first as indicated by the immediate bouncing blue balls of a reply.

"Yes. He's in the office, monitoring the stir you caused." A high-five emoji followed. He could hear the laughter Tristan gave as he sent the message.

"You ready?" Ducky asked from the living room, hovering just beyond the bedroom door. He probably knew what would happen if he came any further inside his room. Ducky looked good in the T-shirt he had given him, which was also now paired with athletic shorts. What he liked the most was the way Ducky wore the ball cap with the brim facing backward. The look fit Ducky's face perfectly.

His traitorous cock plumped. He physically wanted Ducky, but it would have to wait. Besides, he had to prove to himself and Ducky, they were more than just a good lay. They fit together in every part of their lives.

He looked down at his cock, reprimanding its constant need. *You. Will. Wait.*

"Yeah," he finally said in a breathy voice, and lifted his phone, doing a little wave before pulling up his father's contact information, initiating the call. "I'm calling my dad now."

"Come in here." Ducky nodded his head toward the sofa. His innocent look quickly morphed into X-rated when he added that sexy crooked grin.

Chad didn't allow himself to consider the double entendre Ducky used as a suggestion.

His father answered on the first ring.

"I've been worried about you," Dylan Reeves said by way of a greeting.

Chad lifted the phone to better see his father's image. The fine lines of fatigue ringed the sides of his eyes. The guilt that usually followed when dealing with his father tamped down any arousal he'd managed as he followed Ducky's instruction, heading into the living room. "I'm sorry. We just found out the video was out there. Our phones died..."

"That's not what I mean," his dad interrupted, moving his face more predominantly into the phone's screen. "How are you?"

"I'm good, Dad," Chad said, taking the seat on the sofa next to Ducky. He didn't allow an inch of space between them. "Great actually. I wish I could have told you before you saw the video. We didn't know it was posted."

Dylan nodded, still staring intently at Chad but saying nothing more. He could see what Cate said about his father being hurt. He'd been unfair to his dad. Regret caused the truth to tumble from his lips without any further prompting.

"I've been into Ducky for half my life. I just never told anyone. I liked his attitude toward life and that grew into feelings for him. When you came out, it was stunning to me because I'd been hiding for years, but I still couldn't make a move on Ducky. I thought he was straight. It's been a whole head issue thing for me."

"Your mom told me this morning," Dylan said and blew out an unsteady breath as he wiped a hand down his face. "I didn't see this coming. It wasn't on my radar. You two took me by surprise. Tristan feels like I sometimes hover too closely over you and the girls. I'm sorry if that's the case. It's not my intention. I only want you to be happy." His dad's eyes, a mirror image of his own, pinned him in place. "I like Ducky. I've mentioned him to Cate several times. If I had only known I should have been talking to you."

Chad grinned and positioned the phone toward Ducky who lifted a hand in a wave. "Hi, Mr. Reeves. Sorry for all the chaos. We've been unplugged."

The gravity of his father's stare now included Ducky. The same worried expression gave pause before he finally nodded. "Probably the best call for now. How together are you two?"

"Together, together," Chad answered, tilting his head to be visible on the screen with Ducky. He reached for Ducky's hand, threading their fingers together, lifting their joined hands to the phone for his dad to see.

A single nod came again, this time with a smile. "Good. You two are very similar people. Unfortunately, Ducky, I've had to give the approval to ban your brother Donny from Secret. We wiped his entire account. We're tracking his IP address to ensure he doesn't try to come back under a different name. He's been very vocal in his hatred over the last twenty hours. We deemed him dangerous and unstable. He's hitting the tabloids now. They're covering him mainly due to the focus on your new ad campaign. You should probably check in with Dallas."

Ducky's body tensed beside him. "I have Donny blocked on StreamTrainer. Have you done a scan for him there?"

"I did," his father said. "I don't like to breach those boundaries, but you weren't here, and I'm not sure of your office backup..."

"No, sir. You did the right thing." Ducky lifted his cell phone now attached to a power bank to charge. "It's been off, but I see Dallas's messages. I'll call him. I'm sorry we put you in this situation."

Dylan shook his head. "It's fine. Better since I heard from you two."

Ducky nodded again and pushed off the sofa, his phone his focus, his thumbs moving wildly over the screen. "I'm gonna get online."

Chad watched Ducky's retreat to his bedroom. Tension had his back ramrod straight and quickened his steps.

"Thank you, Dad. His brother's an ass," Chad said, finally looking back at his father.

"Back to personal. I'm certainly not one to talk about the secrets anyone holds, but there's pain in hiding. I'm sorry I didn't see this in you sooner."

"Dad, I'm good. It was confusing when I was twelve, but I'm good now. I've been with men before Ducky. I've only hid it from you, Mom, and Chloe."

"So Cate knew?" Dylan asked.

Chad hedged, not wanting to sell out his sister. He finally nodded and grinned. "She's in fashion design, Dad.

It's an open market there." That seemed to explain a lot to his father who laughed and nodded his understanding.

"Tell Ducky he's trending on all social platforms. Modeling agencies are commenting on posts from StreamTrainer, asking if he has an agent. He's famous now."

"Oh God, no," Ducky said loud enough for both he and his father to hear. Chad looked up to see Ducky's horrified expression darting from around the corner of the hall back into the living room. "Dallas just said the same thing."

Chad laughed at the true revelation on Ducky's face. He adjusted the phone's position for his father to see how resistant Ducky was to the idea of a modeling career, or whatever they wanted from him. He looked back to see his father's bright smile. The exhaustion on his face had intensified. It was Chad's undoing. "I was wrong to keep this from you. It's all so personal and private. It was hard to let go of my secrets."

Dylan shook his head, not letting Chad continue. Which wasn't a bad thing, he'd probably grovel an apology for the next hour if given the chance. "I was about your age when I told your mom my truth. We forged a plan to support one another until we could get you guys raised. If it weren't for Tristan, I know I'd still be hiding. You don't have to apologize to me. I'm sorry I wasn't stronger for you. All I've ever wanted is your happiness."

Raw emotion laced each word his father said, causing a lump to form in Chad's throat. "I've always been happy. You've given me a great life. I can say the last twenty-four hours rank as the very best of my life. Duck's been an anchor to me since I first met him." Chad looked away, staring off into the living room, letting the joy of love and friendship fuel his words. "My heart isn't searching anymore. I got what I wanted—a stunningly beautiful, special guy who says he wants to be with me too. I'm good, Dad. Does that make any sense?"

His gaze went back to the screen, his father smiling and nodding. "I get it. I understand completely. That's how I feel about Tristan. Go help Ducky deal with what's on his plate. I'll keep suppressing as much as I can. That's our secret."

Chad absently nodded, feeling the weight of the world lift off his shoulders.

"I'm glad you touched base. Keep your phones on." His dad lifted a hand, waving goodbye, and the screen darkened.

Chad lowered the phone, laying it on his thigh, all his attention landed on Ducky who had stopped feet away. He had to have heard every word Chad said. The concern that had driven him to the living room, melted off his face, leaving nothing but love behind.

Ducky came forward, his cell phone was in his hand but angled in a way that suggested the call might have been forgotten. Chad could hear talking on the other end, but Ducky only focused on Chad. His love leaned down. Warm lips didn't hesitate to press against his. The kiss was so tender and thoughtful that Chad didn't want it to end.

"You good?" Ducky whispered, hovering an inch above his mouth, staring him unabashedly straight in the eyes. With no pretense, only honesty. Genuine love stared at him. They were stronger together, just as Chad had always envisioned them to be.

Chad slid his hand around Ducky's neck, drawing him back for another tender press of lips. The move didn't surprise Ducky, he easily went with it, opening as Chad slanted his mouth, deepening the kiss.

Ducky. The name reverted through his head as if his soul had a voice.

His gamer reared back, ending the sweet embrace. They stared at one another, puffs of breath mingling between them.

"My brother's on the phone," Ducky said and glanced down at the forgotten cell phone still in his hand.

Reality was back in a flash, interrupting their private peaceful paradise. He could hear Dallas's chuckle on the other end of the video call. He looked down to see Dallas's face filling Ducky's phone screen, looking as amused yet concerned as his father had.

He got a playful wink before Ducky took off toward his bedroom.

Crazy-in-love didn't begin to describe all this feeling flowing through him. Chad had no choice but to push up from the sofa and follow Ducky into his room, not wanting to be away from him for a single second. "Wait, I'll go with you."

CHAPTER 21
VIDEOS

Hours after Ducky ventured into the world of StreamTrainer, he tore the headphones off his ears, tossing them onto the desk, and looked up from the workspace he'd created in his bedroom. His laptop sat in the center of the small desk, his phone with the screen facing forward slightly angled to the right, his tablet positioned in the same way to the left. He missed his bank of monitors at the office.

He glanced out the open window toward the ocean, surprised it was already close to dusk. He listened as he stood, stretching his back and shoulders, rolling his neck, hoping to release the tension from being hunched over his equipment. No noise came from inside the villa as he went in search of Chad. Dinner containers rested on the stovetop, closed tight, the smells were delicious.

"You in there?" he called, stopping by Chad's bedroom. He was nowhere to be found.

That something special about their vacation had dimmed over the last few hours. If he were being honest with how bad things were with StreamTrainer because of his brother, Donny, he should probably head back to Texas.

Dylan's concern had seemed overkill until Ducky got a taste of what was happening inside StreamTrainer's social media site. Donny may not have an account on the platform, but his malevolent presence and opinions about the LGBT community had upset the balance of their users. Class participation was down due to an uptick of user comments arguing with one another rather than attending classes, souring the safe place they had worked so hard to achieve.

All hands were on deck in their corporate office. The entire executive team had given up their project loads to be available to assist customer service and their site's monitors fielding all the activity. The entire experience had taxed their already depleted service team.

On the bright side, individual training box orders were up over eight percent from this time last year. On the bad side, his older brother Donny was the lead story on DailyMail and practically every other tabloid site.

Apparently, Donny had found his place in apocalyptic religion over the last year, becoming a born-again believer. He wanted to start his own ministry. His brother's entire religious platform centered on the evils of everything he and Dallas stood for. From their big business goals all the way to the personal decisions both Ducky and Dallas made with their lives.

Obviously, his fundraising efforts grew with every

accusation he sounded off on. Donny was such a whore. Sure, he believed a lot of the venom he spewed, but he'd do or say anything if cash were involved.

The tension in his neck increased again, the muscles clamping down, unerringly reminding him of what had caused these problems. *Money.*

The sounds of the ocean and the billowing curtains from the steady breeze called him to the patio. His heart eased at the sight before him. Maybe he should rethink giving everything away. A place close to the ocean might be the best medicine to unwind from the dysfunctional side of his family.

Chad. The name reverberated through his head like an affirmation, filling all the newly formed cracks from the stress of the last few hours.

His friend and lover came to the forefront of his thoughts, planting himself in the top spot of Ducky's life.

The sudden shift in priorities made Ducky freeze.

That was it!

Everything else was just noise in the background. So at one with the idea of Chad being the most important part of his life that he registered the birds chirping around him, the sweet scent of plumeria trees surrounding the villa, the constant churn of the ocean only feet away.

He was in love with his best friend. Honesty, passion, and friendship all packaged into one complicated emotion. Flutters of desire skidded across his skin. The whisper of Chad's name coursed through every fiber of his body. His entire focus had truly changed.

Chad.

"I don't even know how to have a relationship." Ducky

lifted his face to the sky, speaking his concern to the universe. It didn't seem to matter. He'd figure it out with Chad's help.

Chad supported his decisions.

Chad believed in him. The heavy weight of the last few hours lifted off his shoulders as a calming exhale of breath left his lungs. For the first time in his life, he felt in control, balanced within himself. A big smile spread across his face until it became a chuckle.

His road to change had gone full circle, leading him right back to himself. Perhaps now he understood the ways of the world better. He was definitely more physically and emotionally healthy. Possibly more of a joiner these days, but Chad had managed to bring him back to himself. Back to believing he was good enough the way he was. What a head rush.

He scanned the beach. The bright sand and inviting blue waters went on forever. In the far distance, he spotted Chad jogging toward him. He waved, staring unabashedly at the sight before him. Chad never tired. Endless energy fueled each step. His running shorts and bare chest were a tempting aphrodisiac. All those muscles worked fluidly together. Ducky felt those steps were running to him.

He slipped back inside the rental. If Chad was coming from that direction, he still had half his run to go. Ducky decided to finish the distance with him.

He went for his runners as Donny's bullshit and StreamTrainer fell to the back of his thoughts. With any luck, they'd be completely forgotten by the end of the night.

One month later

"When you told me to give your money away, I didn't realize that meant that I'd have to physically move you." Greer complained as he grabbed one of the moving boxes Ducky pushed to the edge of the U-Haul's trailer. Greer's snippy commentary hadn't abated since he'd shown up at Ducky's apartment, under great duress, with his brother, Dallas, this morning.

Ducky's gaze slid to Chad. His new roommate mumbled something under his breath, showing he was on Greer's exact same page.

"If I'm not being clear, let me add that I would've paid for movers had I known," Greer added, absorbing the heavy weight of the box in his arms.

"It's a few boxes," Dallas said, coming up behind Greer, reaching for another load.

"Yeah." Greer's eyes rolled in a dramatic fashion. "That's the lie you told me this morning to get me to come with you. This U-Haul's full."

Dallas stacked one box on top of another and started back toward the building. "People move all the time. You're supposed to pitch in and help. It's what we do for each other."

"I've never, not one time, moved another human being from their home to another. I don't even move myself." Greer was a dog with a bone. He hadn't stopped his disgruntled grumbling any of the dozens of times he'd come to the edge of the trailer today. He also had no problem with who heard his constant tirade. He spoke his mind with each labored step he took.

Ducky shrugged it off. Since Greer had first come into their lives, being outspoken and getting what he wanted seemed a normal Tuesday for Greer.

"He has a point." Chad grabbed one end of Ducky's heavy desk, his tone a bit gentler than Greer's though. Ducky took the other end, navigating his way off the truck. "I would have gotten us movers."

Ducky let all the strife roll off his shoulders, not letting the aggravation bring his mood down. He had the money for movers. He just couldn't understand paying such a cost with four strong men able to carry the load themselves.

Besides, his and Chad's paradise had carried over into their real everyday lives, fueling the rush of Ducky's move. Every single free minute they had was spent together. Four days ago, they were a melodramatic display at the airport, stalling until the last possible moment before Chad had to tear himself away or miss his flight to California, to make his new position at Wilder permanent. Ducky may or may not have shed a tear or two as he watched Chad take off in a full run toward his gate. He'd missed him with all the same flair and drama of a Shakespearean play until Chad came back home to him.

Ducky wasn't moving into Chad's second bedroom. Those plans had been scrubbed when they landed back on Texas soil from Hawaii. The reality of two separate beds lasted as long as it took for Chad to drive Ducky home from the airport. He made it halfway back to his north Dallas condo before doing a U-turn and coming back to Ducky's place where he'd stayed the night.

When Ducky had opened his front door, Chad had sweetly declared he'd spent too many years convinced he couldn't have what he wanted. Now that they were a couple, Ducky had a lot of TLC makeup work to do. Chad's logic was faulty, and one-sided, but he found himself in complete agreement.

"What're you thinking about?" Chad asked. Ducky tuned back into what they were doing, maneuvering through the side entrance of the building to the service elevator entrance that opened for them. When it came to Chad, his tunnel vision was truly a problem. At least this time, he hadn't walked into oncoming traffic. "I swear your workout pheromones give off a come-fuck-me scent. It's been a little over a month and that blush still does it for me. I'm so screwed."

Chad's head hit the side of the elevator wall and he closed his eyes, still holding the edge of the desk. He said those things all the time, making Ducky feel loved and cherished. "Stop. It's not the time."

"So you say," Chad countered.

"I think yours and Greer's problem is more about the difference of living on the south side versus north side of Dallas." Ducky made the comment on purpose, just to get under Chad's skin, change the direction of the current conversation.

It was an ongoing disagreement over which side of the metroplex was superior. Ducky was firm in his South Dallas ways, only ever consenting to move this far north because of Chad. It seemed a sacrifice for Ducky in both attitude and the intense traffic.

"Omigod, buzzkill. Not the wealthy versus poor thing

again." The diversion seemed to work. Chad stood to his full height, ready to defend his lands.

The elevator dinged, signaling they'd reached their floor. The doors opened as Ducky hoisted up his end of the desk again and started out. Luckily, Chad's place wasn't too far down the hall from the service elevator. "I wasn't talking about class structure. I was talking about helping your neighbors. We're better at it down there."

The gauntlet was officially thrown.

Chad's shocked outrage had him pushing against Ducky a little faster than he'd like to walk with such a heavy load. "We help our neighbors up here. You're a money snob, Ducky. I can't believe you think so little of where I grew up."

Normally Ducky could hold his laughter a bit longer when Chad's back unjustifiably bowed up, but Dallas appeared in Chad's front doorway, jumping out of the way, holding the door open to help Ducky navigate inside.

"What's so funny?" Dallas asked.

"Listening to Chad defend himself as a rich kid," Ducky explained and laughed harder as Chad's petulance increased.

Instead of taking the desk to the spare bedroom, now an office for the both of them, Chad stopped in the living room, just off the entry, dumping the desk there. Chad stalked around the edge, his menacing stare made Ducky hold his ground, eager for whatever was about to happen.

"I'm gonna fuck you over this desk for that comment," Chad whispered only for his ears to hear, grabbing him by the hips, tugging him flush against his hard body. "You just think you like it hard. I'm going to show you what a rich kid can do."

"Promise?" Ducky challenged. Yeah, he definitely wanted Chad to follow through on his vow.

"Do they know we can hear them?" Greer asked, strolling past him and Chad on his way to the front door.

On the descent for a kiss, mere inches from Ducky's mouth, Chad stopped and announced boldly, "I don't care if they can hear because it's gonna happen. Fact." Chad's smiling lips met his.

"Video it," Greer called out, not sounding shocked in the least. "I promise you'll love watching it just as much later."

"Greer, that's my little brother," Dallas said defensively, almost angrily, as he followed Greer out the door. Neither his brother nor brother-in-law bothered with shutting it behind them, probably for fear Chad planned to execute his promise once they were alone.

His embarrassed gaze collided with Chad's. Not because of Greer, but more in worry that the video idea might take root in Chad's head, and they'd quickly amass a collection of private viewing material.

"What, Dallas? You know I love watching our home videos," Greer said loudly in the distance. Of course being inappropriate changed Greer's mood for the better.

"You don't just announce it to everyone out loud," Dallas countered heatedly. "It's private."

"I didn't say what we did in the videos. I just offered them a tip on how to make things…interesting." Greer's chuckling voice faded until it could no longer be heard.

"No video," Ducky said. That was a hard pass for him. He saw way too many ways that could go wrong.

"Yeah, no video. We'll live stream," Chad teased, before taking his lips again. The quick, hot kiss curled Ducky's toes. The scent of his hot, sweaty guy mixed with that sexy cologne had Ducky deepening the kiss for a few seconds longer.

"I'm glad you're here," Chad said, pressing his forehead against Ducky's.

"Same," Ducky whispered and leaned in to kiss Chad again.

EPILOGUE

Six months later

"It's essential to know exactly where you are in the air compared to the water you're falling into," Kruger Towns, the newly signed Wilder Sports diver explained to Chad. It was hard to know who was more excited about his three-day crash course into the world of amateur cliff diving, him or Kruger, but he found himself jonesing to take his first dive doing something other than tombstoning straight into the water.

He nodded his understanding, analyzing in his mind the fifty-foot pike jump he planned to make. As high as it felt standing there on the edge looking down into the water, it was considered a low dive to the professionals. Kruger jumped eighty feet and higher regularly.

"Keep your vertical position in line with the water. You're gonna crush it," Kruger encouraged. The diver stuck out a hand for a quick, encouraging dap-slap.

He and Ducky had arrived in Krabi Province, Malaysia, a little over two days ago. Chad had become a globe trekker over the last few months, running after all the talent he wanted to sign to Wilder Sports. This trip, though, had been planned strategically to add a couple of extra days so he and Ducky had time together to do what they wanted. He'd signed Kruger within a couple of hours of arriving then spent the remaining time using Kruger as a coach, learning how to cliff dive properly.

"I keep my chin even, like it's on a shelf," Chad said absently, mentally ticking off the movements he had to hit in the five or six seconds he was in the air. He took the time to stretch his back and shoulders before mimicking the super aligned pose of the divers he'd watched. "I'm doing a pike this time."

"Correct," Kruger said, back to all business as he moved closer to the very edge of the protruding cliff for a safer dive. "And he's jumping today?"

Kruger's chin tilted toward Ducky, sitting quietly a few feet away where he'd planted himself over the last several days. Ducky rarely spoke but this wasn't like the moments of meditation by the ocean in Hawaii. Ducky stayed attentive and focused, watching and listening to everything around him.

His gamer was getting back to his old self, at least if his hair was any indicator. The curls were back, and Chad loved them. Ducky sat with his muscular arms wrapped around his knees. He had a deep tan—Chad's doing. They spent more time in the sun than in the gym, just the way Chad liked it.

Ducky wore a ball cap and sunglasses today. The dark curls sprang out the sides and the brim, refusing to be contained.

"It's high," Ducky called out.

Chad gave a pointed stare over his shoulder, locking on Ducky's pouty lips.

"You promised you'd do a jump. There's seriously nothing to fear. You'll love the adrenaline rush. All you have to do is what they taught us. We practiced this morning," Chad said in a rush of words. Ducky had opened his willingness to try new things. His boyfriend was the whole reason they extended their time here on this trip. Ducky was a pro diving off the high board at the swimming pool. He could do this with no problem, and Chad wanted to share the experience with him. "This is your last chance. Trust me. You're gonna want to be diving all the time after this."

Chad turned back to Kruger and nodded on Ducky's behalf. "He wants to try. He's just nervous. Talk him through it like you do me. I'll stay at the bottom and meet him down there."

He'd already broken all professional boundaries, insisting this diving team teach him how to properly cliff dive. If they were home, Chad knew how to ease Ducky's anxiety. He'd done those things early this morning. Ducky had this.

He extended a hand to Ducky, doing a quick motion with his fingers. "Come here. Watch me. Tell me what I need to change." He heard the pleading in his voice and the not so silent chuckle from Kruger's coach, standing in the distance. Whatever. Ducky wanted to dive. He'd help him with the courage part. "They're going to bring our stuff down. Take off your shirt. Get ready. We got this. Come down right after me."

Ducky stood, doing as Chad asked. He removed his ball cap and sunglasses. The tank top followed. "Be careful. It's high. Watch the water," Ducky said, handing his belongings to the coach.

"*Pfft*. It's only high the first time," Chad teased then swung back toward the ocean. He stared at the hypnotic motion of the small waves and cleared all thought from his head. His body vibrated with excited energy. His training took over, the actions drilled into him. He extended his arms, taking a deep breath.

"You got this," Ducky encouraged quietly. His soul responded, giving a full body flush of adrenaline as he released the breath and jumped. A smile spread across his face as his feet left solid ground and the breeze flew over his body.

His life was perfect.

⟋

Ducky leaned over the rocky edge, watching Chad execute the roll he'd practiced before aligning himself with the water and dropping in. Of course, the dive was perfect. He'd been dumb to worry for Chad for even a second.

"Here you go," Kruger said from behind Ducky, handing him back his shirt. Ducky yanked on the tank, stepping several inches from the edge, watching Chad get congratulations from those watching on the shore below.

When Chad looked up, he gave a giant arm swing wave from the ocean, wanting Ducky to join him.

Yeah right, like that was ever going to happen. Ducky took the ball cap and sunglasses back. He added those to his face and head as he started for the jeep. Kruger followed behind him. "I thought when you asked if I was going to jump that you blew it."

"Nah," Kruger said as if he knew exactly what he was doing. "He watches you all the time. He'd have asked if I hadn't. Then you'd have to lie. This way, you never really confirmed. It's all on me."

Ducky only grunted a reply. Nice try, but Kruger, and the coach for that matter, hadn't watched as he'd beg for release this morning when Chad held him off until he'd promised to dive today. He let that bit of information go unsaid.

"He's gonna be pissed," the coach said, sliding into the driver's side of the jeep. The whole experience seemed hilarious to both the coach and Kruger, based on the way they cackled. Pissed wasn't quite the emotion he expected to get when he saw Chad next. Probably more like disappointment, concern, or super attention as he tried to pinpoint Ducky's exact reservation and fix it.

"He'll get over it. I do this all the time," Ducky said, taking the front passenger seat. Kruger jumped in the back seat. "At some point, he's gonna figure out I'm more a watcher than a participant."

Kruger bowled over in the backseat, laughing uproariously.

"Don't bet on it. My wife says I never learn," the coach said.

Ducky was perfectly fine with that. It spoke sweetly to his heart with how badly Chad wanted him to experience all the things he loved. But diving fifty feet didn't bode well for his intense fear of heights. It was damn hard to walk to the cliff's edge and look over. He felt that was accomplishment enough for this adventure.

"It took me time, but I figured out who you were," Kruger's hand clasped his shoulder from behind. "You're the guy in the fitness commercials."

Luckily Kruger couldn't see his eye roll behind his sunglasses. He was never going to live down those ads.

Unfortunately, the drive down didn't take much more time than the dive itself. When they took the last curve, he spotted Chad on the back of a jet ski, coming to shore.

Their gazes locked as Chad received his congratulations. His boyfriend gave nods of appreciation, otherwise ignoring everyone other than Ducky.

"What the hell, Reigns?" Chad called out, still dripping water. Ducky grinned, not feeling one ounce of remorse in his decision to ride down with Kruger and the coach rather than fling himself off the cliff. He watched as Chad stalked toward him. The jeep barely came to a stop before Kruger jumped out from the back, the coach grinding the gear shift in place before he exited the jeep. They clearly expected something raw and rough to go down.

"I'm afraid of heights," Ducky explained with patience in his tone.

"But you wanted this," Chad countered, coming to his side of the jeep.

"Did I?" Ducky replied, looking as quizzical as Chad looked certain.

Chad's face went through a range of emotion before he busted a move, leaping straight into his seat, landing on Ducky's lap. In the same motion, Chad grabbed Ducky, dousing him in unexpectedly chilly water.

He was so unprepared for the move, he did little more than spit and sputter as Chad rubbed his cheek and water-soaked hair along Ducky's face. Water splashed everywhere, covering him head to toe.

"You're wet. Get off me," Ducky said the obvious and pushed at his irritating boyfriend, but he couldn't help the chuckle at the unexpected drenching.

Chad wasn't going anywhere. He wrapped his strong arms around Ducky, holding him pinned against the seat and his body. As the youngest, smallest brother, he'd learned a long time ago how to outmaneuver this particular hold, but he refused to take advantage of that particular extraction skill in this instance. He loved the man holding him so tightly.

"I'm starting to get the idea that you're a *yes* man in name only," Chad said, pulling back enough that maybe six inches separated their faces. He had no idea how long the honeymoon phase of a relationship lasted, but he was deep in the throes of their chemistry. He continued to react to Chad as if he was the hottest, most endearing guy on the planet…which he was, so it worked out great.

When Chad's gaze focused on his lips, Ducky's cock plumped, taking his guy's brows up in surprise. "I'm reprimanding you. You're not supposed to like it."

"Mmm. Watching you be a daredevil is my favorite. Did you love the jump?" Ducky moved to place a small kiss on Chad's lips. One he followed when Ducky tried to move away.

"I love it, but not as much as I love you," Chad said, slanting his mouth over Ducky's to deepen the kiss.

"Pay up," he heard Kruger say at a distance.

"Jeez," the coach replied, disgruntled. "Reeves is whopped. That argument should have lasted at least five minutes. Do they ever stop kissing?"

Chad lifted only a fraction of an inch, speaking almost against Ducky's lips. "Ignore them. They're jealous I got you first. How about a pizza, some beer, and a night in so you can ease my bruised feelings?"

"Deal," Ducky answered without hesitation.

His boyfriend sealed the commitment with another quick peck before deftly twisting. In one fluid motion, Chad landed in the driver's side of the vehicle, quickly starting the engine. The wicked gleam in his eye shared the promise of what was to come.

"Hey," Kruger called out as Chad did a mini burnout of revved engines and a sand cloud behind them. "Don't leave us here."

"Use the money you just made to get home." Who knew if Kruger heard him or not? But the hands planted on his hips and the coach's loud laughter showed they got the gist.

Chad drove the getaway vehicle with more speed than necessary. As he moved the gearshift around, his pinky finger reached for Ducky's, hooking around his as he continued to shift, creating more speed.

Ducky grabbed the roll bar, holding on as he looked back at the dust cloud behind them. It seemed the perfect example of their lives, leaving everything that didn't matter in the rearview mirror. Chad looked over at Ducky, grinning wildly. He returned the smile and sat back in his seat, ready for the ride of his life.

The End

NOTE FROM THE AUTHOR

Send a quick email to kindle@kindlealexander.com and let us know what you think of Level Up. For more information on future works, sign-up for our new release newsletter at www.kindlealexander.com or come friend us on all the major social networking sites.

BOOKS BY KINDLE ALEXANDER

If you enjoyed **Level Up** then you won't want to miss Kindle Alexander's bestselling novels:

Breakaway
Reservations
It's Complicated
Painted On My Heart
The Current Between Us (with Bonus Material)
Closet Confession
Secret
Texas Pride
Full Disclosure
Double Full
Full Domain
Always
Forever
Havoc
Order

The Reigns Brothers Books
Breakaway
Level Up
Reading order Secret, Breakaway, Level Up

A Reservation Story
Reservations Book 1
It's Complicated Book 2
Reading order of all the characters mentioned in A
Reservation Story Series
Secret, Painted On My Heart, Reservations, It's Complicated

Always & Forever Duet
Always
Forever

Nice Guys Novels
Double Full
Full Disclosure
Full Domain

Tattoos and Ties
Havoc
Order
Reading order of all the characters mentioned in Tattoos and
Ties. Up In Arms, Painted On My Heart, Havoc, Order

Better If Read Together
The Current Between Us
Secret
Painted On My Heart
Reservations
It's Complicated